MANHATTAN

T0017356

MANHATTAN

LETTERS FROM PREHISTORY

HÉLÈNE CIXOUS

Translated by Beverley Bie Brahic

An imprint of Fordham University Press
New York   2023

Originally published in French as *Manhattan: Lettres de la préhistoire* copyright 2002 Éditions Galilée.

This work has been published with the assistance of the National Center for the Book–French Ministry of Culture.

Ouvrage publié avec le soutien du Centre national du livre–ministère français chargé de la culture.

Visit us online at https://www.fordhampress.com/new-york-relit/.

CONTENTS

This is not a dead object but an underground explosion whose seismic, personal, and literary consequences still continue to make themselves felt.

Just how difficult it is to speak of it as book in the rubble you shall see.

This explosion, mental maybe and cultural, takes place in 1965 in the rare manuscript collections of the libraries of Yale, Buffalo, and Columbia universities, and in Manhattan's enchanted locations, in Central Park, around the Statue of Liberty.

These places have powers of fascination, herein termed "omnipotence-others," for, as far as New York's history and physiognomy are concerned, they are exactly like *The Odyssey*'s fateful locations (the entrance to Hades, where the act of spilling blood calls up the forever still living dead; Mount Circeo, where human beings, of old and still today, are changed to pigs and vice versa, before this happens all over again in the Gospels). These strangely real locations whose monumental forms rise up into the American air, Grand Central Station whose vault covers the sky, where anything in the world can happen—from the beginning of love to a crime or the end of the world—have roots that reach deep, right down to the passions' infernos, right to the ocean bottoms of memory.

Stroll here at your own risk. From the beginning these places have been inhabited by memories of demons and dreams.

People have come here to die to resuscitate, to disappear, to disappear once and for all or to reappear—as here—in a tale, since the eighteenth century, since *Manon Lescaut,* not forgetting Karl Rossmann, the character in Kafka's *Amerika*, and a great buddy of Benjamin Jonas, who was my grandmother's little brother.

Among all the Jonas in search of the Whale in whose belly to carry out the rites of Banishment, there was in those days a certain Gregor, the really fabulous and unfathomable character of this attempt at a tale.

One day in 1964 in Manhattan, at the turn of a destiny very young and already marked by the repeated deaths of loved ones always called George, between the young woman who loved literature more than anything else in the world and the young man whose mind was a copy of the most bewitching works of the Library, the fatal Accident occurs.

The fateful primal scene, the "evil eye" scene, happens *in reality* (just as if it had been written by Edgar Poe) in a tombstone of a library at Yale. Sometimes for a speck of dust in your eye the world is lost.

After this, everything happens very very fast for, like the Lovers, the taxi of the mad careers downhill to Hell faster than water throwing itself into a gorge.

Literature as Omnipotence-other, the invented Idol, is the main other-character of this adventure. Literature corroded our powers of reasoning the way the USA gobbles up your gray matter.

Everything takes place in the before-work, a prehistoric season when the characters, smitten with great dead authors, see themselves as books already, as volumes in their dreams, stealing up on the dreamed "Oeuvre," stealthy as wolves, on tiptoe like fools—closing in on the adored Author by Imitation, tracing paper, magic introjection. The copycat "does" Kafka, turns himself into Kafka, from *A* to *Z* commits Kafka suicide, right up to the spitting of blood, right up to the deathbed scene.

Now enter the third character in this tempest: *The Letter,* prehistory of all literature, a supplementary oeuvre, or rather *maneuver.* "The letters someone writes you," wrote Proust, "draw a sufficiently different image of the person you know for them to constitute a second personality." Letters: feints. Soon, the second personality totally supplants the person, who is at bottom really no one, nothing but a little two-bit character, less substantial than Elpenor (who? "Elpenor," a nobody member of Ulysses's crew, dead without ever having lived, at the age of twenty-seven). The second personality now gleams with all his tragic fires. We have eyes only for Him, this god, improvised hero, dazzling, inaccessible, this all but incredible Gregor.

In point of fact we are eyeless and godless. I can't tell true from false any more, the simulacrum from the reality. I believe what one doesn't believe. One sees what one doesn't see. I don't love whom I love or maybe I love whom I don't love. The Word takes absolute power over the senses. Literature wins, it casts its powers of illusion over the world, into the streets, into the veins of time, over the skin of the body. What is "written" is. What is is not. Naturally it's unbearable for the person who has lived through the Manhattan brazier to return to the scene of literary dementia. Every time I try to call up room 91 of the King's Crown Hotel where these spellbinding scenes were acted alive, I renounce, I am lightningstruck all over again.

MANHATTAN

CERTES A SACRIFICE

I didn't want to go to Certes and there I was on my way side by side with my brother I'm forever doing what I didn't want to do I thought I am in a state of sin it is Easter the first day of passing over instead of passing over to my side I pass to the other—looklook how beautiful it is my brother was saying I looked

the boats on their sides in the silted up channel slack time the sea has withdrawn we make our way between hundreds of tipped hulls I see them as dead I see them as tuna gasping for breath, a posthumous landscape. I found it unbeautiful, a still life, the graveyard scene, from my brother's perspective: the simple life devoid of unpleasantness the empty hour invisible fishermen gone to lunch says my brother

I am in a state of sin I always do what I didn't want to do, right away I do *everything* I didn't want to do, sin spreads out over my whole heart, on all sides a feeling of being sucked into the mud grips my thoughts, the square notebook tucked into the left pocket of my shirt weighs on my heart as if it too were quickened by regret, on my right on my brother's side too I am in a state of sin

We walk side by side Pierre walks I sin on all sides, him dry shod me in mud

each time I've wanted to get back to writing and I've wanted to write *at all costs* I have left the book behind, I have even left my own life behind and entered a country I didn't want to be in,

at the very moment writing, the right, the country, the visa had been granted me after having been taken away and forbidden me for years, the very day "my life" as I call literature had been given back to me, the other, "life," suggests I go the other way, and I go, I can't help it, it's stronger than my desire, this other desire I am, a ghost I don't see bars my life and the very day I wanted *at all costs to go to my life* I go to *the other*.

To think it took me forty years to discover Certes on my doorstep my brother was saying you've got thirty kilometers of road between the salt ponds, it's extraordinarily beautiful, he exults in his discovery and I am in a state of sin I was thinking I'm losing New York to the salt ponds I thought I was going to get there today thirty-five years it's taken me to get to the New York book, looklook this virginal sky in which I see feeble flickers of Manhattan's skyscrapers drowning, the huge simulacra that had so fascinated me getting covered up by the heart-rending softness of Certes' silk

once again I do what I didn't want to do and it is I nonetheless therefore an other who is doing this to me I thought the personal pronoun has been betrayed I came here to write The Story, as we call this book that is slipping out of my grasp, this very day was stamped on my calendar months ago I've been through weeks of quarantine I've put up with boredom fear inanition thanks to this day's date, knowing the name of the day of deliverance is itself a release, finally it comes, Time keeps its word, the door to my mental prison swings open, and me does not come out, I am not in my life, I catch the plane for the book, but instead of finding myself safe and sound at my desk, I see myself in reality on the road to Certes walking to the left of my brother like a madwoman, like some hostility come out of my back, a wicked angel puts me in my place legs unsteady leaning on my brother whom I love I drag myself to the rack without admitting it, it's not that I am giving in to my brother it's worse than that, murkier, I myself lock myself up outside myself, I make myself *flee*, I do exactly *what I didn't want to do* and not what my brother wanted, I don't even do what my brother wants but what my opposite wants although (1) clearly I did not want to go on this outing to Certes (2) for seven months I've been waiting *at all costs* for this day to come, awaiting it for decades but less wholeheartedly, and now the day goes by without me in front of me, a cool, healthy, breezy April day, I could jump, take it on the run, my brother isn't forcing me, when I told him as we arrived in Certes I don't want to go to Certes he responded tactfully we'll go wherever you want. We took the road away from Certes, toward the Ocean. Where the road crossed the highway I said: let's go to Certes. And my brother took the direction away from the Ocean. He was happy to do as I wished, but the sin was already sinning in all directions again, against me against my brother, against my will. What's left of my will is in my left breast pocket the little notebook which throbs, against my heart—divided, like a heart. I seem crazy to myself I see clearly that nothing is clear in my confusion, supposing I speak to my brother who will it be speaking to him?

* * *

I am still astounded by the violence of my reactions, I tell myself. You run along between the strings of boats lying like so many dead fish, clinging to your brother as if you dreamt the end of the world might catch up with you in Certes. Certes is nothing but a hole after all. You are astounded? I am astounded by your astonishment. Didn't you yourself wake her up, the one whose presence or absence you so dread?

And that was thanks to your brother, unintentionally, with his unintentional help. He's a doctor after all, unintentionally, but still.

She who was running like a madwoman between two rows of inert bodies because, or so she thought, she was in danger of losing her mind and felt she should make her way to the exit as fast as possible was the same me whom I had lost or who had lost me violently, brutally, in the USA in 1965, she who was me, a liberated woman, strong, solid, proud of descending from my sensible mother, having inherited her sense of direction, which had suddenly persuaded me to plunge into the absolutely interminable labyrinth that snakes under the City of New York, I'm not interested I said whereupon I nevertheless found myself winding through kilometers of underground tunnels, kilometers of gut tiled in bizarrely shaped white terracotta, sometimes standing up often bent beneath the too-low ceiling, sometimes flattened so as to glide like a letter through the slot, it would take weeks, I've got other things to do I said they're waiting for me in my country, I have children, a family, which way to the exit I asked. Exit? You have to find it, if there is one. In thirty-five kilometers said the advertising voice, male, husky and encouraging. Few people know the underground. How did I get there? Special delivery. Recommended. Like that last letter, addressed to New York, to New York in person, by this me, encysted or so I'd thought after 1965's abscess, but in

4

fact merely dormant and always ready to wake up a demon since the day she'd totally done me in, swiftly and violently, in 1964, a blow or two in New Haven to start then in Buffalo, then right after that and fatally in New York, this me lodged in the seismic depths of me, inactive for decades, then capable of crushing everything without warning some night, had committed the suicidal error of turning back to Certes when, to please me, my brother had given up the idea, perhaps *because he had given it up*, without our realizing that in doing so he was giving free reign and unhoped-for encouragement to my annihilation urge.

I thought of her, my fearsome; I think: she's on the rampage. This strength, tangled up in my roots, which is perhaps one of my roots, never gives me time to talk back. She's a bolt from the blue. One of those "other powers," those omnipotence-others on whom Proust and his mental denizens must have bestowed this vague enigmatic and therefore terrifying and utterly essential name during the havoc wrought by the passage of Hurricane Albertine. They are unleashed in the cataclysm. They are us, we don't know them, once they're on the loose it is best to face the truth: we haven't the strength to tame the *omnipotence-others*. The solution—medicine, acknowledging their superiority whenever it meets up with them—abdicates reason and consents to a mad collaboration, says the soul doctor. Intelligence reasonably sides with madness. Abdicate, I told myself, such in its wisdom is folly's advice. I was having a problem with this. In my little logbook I wrote the word: *abdication*. Lacking a cure words rush to the rescue.

In tiny letters I scribbled: "The first time I abdicated was that famous first of January 1965 in New York there was a snowstorm, I was astray just as *the world* (the whole world) was astray."

Reasonably, I abdicated reason, I conceded the superiority of the omnipotence-others.

These other-powers came on the one hand from the other-realm, on the other hand from a world that has always had absolute power over me: *literature.*

These lines fit on a page of the Idea notebook 5 x 5 with little squares, the smallest you can find. My ideas-on-the-run must therefore fit this format. I note my brother standing up me hunched on a stump, Gulf to Certes road.

Idea miniaturizes the violence of my flashes.

Another sample Idea: note of April 1, 2001:

Right away after the disappearance
of my son George
I left Bordeaux
and right after that
Paris as well as the whole rest of France
Where my three friends
G(eorge) G(eorge) and G(eorge)
Remained, without news of me.
Besides it was only
much later I noticed
(to tell the truth last year)
the coincidence of the names

What I like about my brother I was thinking is his doctor's presence, there's a doctor in my brother, walking along beside him I am aware of the doctor at my side, this allows me to be sick, at my brother's side I am in the place of illness but mental, but shyly it's not something I boast about, still this is understood in our conversations and in our silences, in our intensely chaste complicity, that it is not impossible for the human being to be mental, to be mentally strong or weak, strength is weakness and vice versa in this domain is something we never discuss but whose existence as a hazy and undeniable region in our vicinity, we have acknowledged from the beginning of time

we never mention it, but still surreptitiously between us there's a password of sorts, the bizarre name of *Clos-Salembier*, often we say Clos-Salembier, as if we were speaking of the Algiers neighborhood in which the two of us were shut up and nailed down together over forty years ago but these vocables are loaded with implications whose explicit inventory we have never compiled,

to say "Clos-Salembier" is to suggest and invoke several successive universes all endowed with anguish fury and excitement. From time to time "I find myself back in the Clos-Salembier" says my brother and we know. Whenever my brother says "I find myself back in the Clos-Salembier" I know he is lost, surrounded and embattled, and me too consequently for the one drags the other down with him and vice versa. The minute I say "I find myself back in Manhattan" we are prey to exaltation. We say "I find myself," this means I am lost, lost in the unfathomable depths of some incarceration whose keys we cannot locate.

But in another way it is only fenced in the Clos, in the jagged confinement, in the Salembrian bites and lacerations that my brother finds *himself*, a kind of reflexivity that only his self-portrait gives back to him and me too therefore, if he finds himself forever there too I find myself assailed, me with the same with my brother chained as if by enchainment, for in the Clos, the enchantment was caused and redoubled by the enchainment, we were *never without chains*, especially our lives' two essential chains: (1) the chain of the dog, our one and only dog, the soul, the angel of our daily outing; (2) the chain of the gate to which all the time the whole spirit of our destiny (which we only knew later) was linked and all the family ties, above all the supreme tie with our beloved wizard, the figure of our young father, forever and to this day sublimated, the key to heaven's constellated gate, the cover of The Book, the gods' frail shadow on earth, the born-revenant, always already a revenant even when he wasn't dead, always ghostly and never really there, even at home he was somewhere else to our two alert minds it was obvious he came back to us from profound sojourns among the dying the dead and the ill including the mad. But we never breathed a word of this not me to my brother nor vice versa. We called this delectably ghostly sensation "Clos-Salembier" (*Manhattan* in English). My father was a madman according to my mother to this day she can't fathom how having such authority being so princely, reigning over the apartments and the whole family and beyond, how being waited on first by his mother granny my grandmother just like the *sacerdos* to whom she served a bowl of couscous each time she made couscous, for him and him alone, descending in majesty from the fourth floor on which she lived to the third floor where my father had made his home, thus bringing from the higher floor to the lower which was highest of all because it sheltered her son our father and in third place my mother's husband, and then being *waited on* by Omi my maternal grandmother along with my mother, and then obeyed and worshipped by us, how on earth this holy saintly never questioned extremely authoritarian doctor could always right up to the day of his death have been so credulous, credulous to the point of death, to dying of it, absolutely, absurdly confident in—it struck me as completely idiotic says my mother, yourfather the idiot, at my age I don't feel the need to hide what I think and always with great vigor and clarity, it's too bad it's the age at which the past grows a little vague but my judgment sharp as ever: Myfather the idiot was worshipped as lord of the manor *everything handed to him* on a silver platter and in a golden cup, my wizard father.

—How can you trust someone who has confidence in everyone? This question will dog my mother to her dying day. Myfather was idiotic in the First War some blindly idealistic people were enthusiastic about *sacrificing themselves,* says my mother, I have no idea what my enthusiastic-to-the-end father thought I haven't yet figured out whether he believed he owed Germany something, someone ought to have told him: *Charity begins at home,* my extraordinary but nonetheless war-idiot of a father yourfather had the same flaw, despite being considerably more authoritarian than me, yet another war-blind the Second one, yourbrother too tortuous thinking appeals to him, communism, what an idea not one I've ever had illusions about, flaws in reasoning suddenly you're at war men believe in it being basically much more authoritarian than the average, I still haven't figured out whether they believed or whether they believed they should believe.

You too eyes shut always full of confidence blinded by confidence to the point of believing in that shady American. You inherited the intelligence of my Hungarian grandfather on my father's side who used to rise at five in the morning and read the Talmud. You rise at five to read but the woman who goes around the farm on horseback and has no faith in anything is me. One cannot read without believing: you read you believe.

—It's not all right I thought, it's not going to be all right, I tell myself, I can walk along beside my brother as much as I like, we're not in step, the ungluing has begun, the ancient unavowable persecution, I keep my feet moving one after the other while underneath it's sizzling, the doubling up has begun. Don't think about it I thought, it'll stop, stick to your brother, don't think about not thinking, stick, stick, stick

—Look at those people says my brother, looklook-at-them-those-people-over-there I love them my brother exclaims, directing my gaze at a group of hikers that my brother contemplates ecstatically, look at them hiking and not harming anyone, trooping along toward the salt ponds, see how lovely it is, I looked and saw the troop, beings of all ages and shapes, having boots and backpacks in common, naked calves of all sizes and degrees of hairiness as well, some with walking sticks with all sorts of hairdos some with gray or greasy or no hair at all looklook how beautiful they are says my brother, I'm looklooking I say I don't believe in it, I thought, I have no faith in hiking, I looked at the hikers and saw them as I was supposed to see them and I go on seeing them as they are I thought, ugly awkward cheerful about as lovely as Hieronymus Bosches in the self-destructive state into which I was sinking as I snaked along beside my brother

looklook how they glow with health, how good human nature is out of doors, my brother rejoiced, meanwhile I was thinking just the opposite I have lost all contact with the medical world, he reiterated, each time we go for a walk, he makes a point of saying this, as if to renew a vow made despite himself. The hospital? I go up the stairs. I'm tightening the screws. If I'm still on staff there three days a week it merely goes to prove I have totally broken with them, at the hospital I'm tightening the screws.

It is certainly true that my brother no longer wants to be a doctor, not ever again, I'm leaning on the doctor he himself has dismissed, whom I keep safe as we wend our way back up the slippery slopes, I slide my arm into the ring of my brother's arm and I prop my stumbling thoughts on the doctor-in-hiding-driven-out on his own orders, he claims his medical past was a long state of wandering for decades he wandered playing the medicine-man, day after day for thirty years he saw himself in a lab coat and stethoscrope *in vicissitude* he says, right up to the day he tears the coat off and throws down his stethoscope, *for you must throw it,* into the trash, a gesture no doctor has ever before committed, a gesture one may take as comic but which I cannot conceive of without shuddering, tears come to my eyes at the thought of this smashing of the icon, at the thought of this cruel inflicting but courageous but cruel

I picture myself throwing down my pen, the one I am gripping between the three live fingers of my right hand right here right now which I love like the flesh of my pet cat, this pen which waits for me and breathes life into me and vice versa I picture myself as my brother flinging it to the ground, deliberately, and cutting it off from me along with the three fingers it is attached to and that desire it and squeeze it as a blind man his stick of light and it's as if I pictured myself in a moment of great madness putting out my own eye the one that reads in other words my right hand, and in order to do so having reached that state of total dissociation which renders self-mutilation possible; and seeing myself commit such madness I want to run away from myself, I want to drag myself away, I want to crack open my head and take out the brain

the way I see it my brother has committed or accomplished or executed the most terrible act of all, he has driven the doctor out of himself therefore health, sense, authority, science, wisdom, and even philosophy itself, he has divided himself up, accused judged expelled all or parts

nothing more shattering and spectacular, confronted with this suicidal and homicidal act I feel aghast with admiration before what I myself would have been incapable of doing without dying on the spot, what I cannot conceive of myself doing except from a distance, in my imagination and with the help of an intermediary, the way I see it my brother has done this,

which is why since the smashing he has taken on the strange dimensions of a hero, somewhat larger than himself, somewhat out of himself, somewhat beyond himself. I stand before him in admiration of this flaying of the flesh, this laying bare of bone and tendon, this live cutting up of his life's greater part.

The way he sees it what I call suicide is a vital triumph, a miraculous birth at the age of fifty-five, a crushing of the enemy within, breaking the bonds of a servitude liable to drag on to the end of his days. Him roused from his nightmare story, me clutching his arm asleep.

"Did I spend any days other than the first of January 1965 in the Manhattan Hotel whose name I have not forgotten nor the exact layout of room and bath? I don't remember. It was blanketed in extreme snow, everything enveloped in the snow that devours traces and curtains off the scene. The Hotel at least really exists. Check it out." I wrote this as I walked along beside my brother on April 1, 2001. Thinking I was haunted. Embarrassingly. But who knows which plot is main, which secondary? One date does not the past make.

As for my brother: is the past ever past?

For me a doctor is a doctor the secret synonym for the brother I clutch as I go under for the first time while for him the thought of being a doctor is threat of death. I've been banished from my life for fifty-five years I wasn't born. *Banishment* I thought the note of banishment rings true, no greater suffering than banishment, the worst being self-banishment naturally, I thought now that I found myself back in my study having felt during the whole brief interminable time in Certes that I would never be back again, I'd suffered a crisis of exile, meanwhile my brother hadn't stopped celebrating his own flight out of Egypt. Still, I thought, my anguish was caused by the mere shadow of self-banishment, which is all it takes as we know to set off the crisis—right away it went to extremes, and similarly the note of satisfaction in the voice of my brother who, every time we go for a walk, gives himself a pat on the back for having shrugged off the yoke after fifty-five years of suffering, rang excessively loud. The theme of *banishment* unites us I thought, the one believing herself banished the other delivered, the shadow of banishment stepped up to join our two shadows on the road to Certes.

Besides that same evening of Certes I noticed, as I was trying to untangle the knotted skein of this catastrophe by holding my pen very straight, nearly vertical the better to jab its beak into the middle of the knots, I see from a glance at my desk that what with the shock of my brother's self-butchery and, on the rebound, of my own hypersensitive imagination, I am unable to contain my story on a single page, and in just one hour I went after it—on one, two, three, four of six sheets of paper, I even had to crack open three brand-new notebooks or writing pads of different sizes one after another in my flight, ripping off the cellophane packaging as a fugitive throws herself first on one bank then on the other with an animal instinct for survival.

And so on the extremely narrow path between the mortuary mounds with their strings of gutted boats, I'd been gripped by the certitude that, in having let myself be sidetracked to Certes,

I had played and lost my writing destiny, and no one but myself
to blame

the word sacrifice, I thought,

the word sacrifice is totally foreign to me, I told myself, yet it
gets its hooks into me, a word with frantic fingernails, I regret
everything it suggests with a primitive disgust, I see the slaugh-
ter of sheep or rams and I want to vomit, I see crazy offerings
and I quiver furiously, all this innocent blood drunk by the
linens, the fleeces, the calicos, silk, wood, kings, madmen I
thought I hate the bloody madmen I thought, I flee from the
imbibers of blood

the word sacrifice remains, the sacrifice remains, the word,

useless to try and scare it off, I mused, I could tell it was still
hanging on there in a dim corner of an ancient memory I never
go near, associated with sacred animals with whom I have la-
mentable affinities. "Sacrifice" is someone I'd like to have swept
away with a violent broom but I haven't done it, a terrible compassion stays my hand through a film of tears in the grubbiest,
least visited, most avoided corner of my darkness I catch sight
of a small swarm of denied creatures among whom pell-mell
the unrecognizable or unrecognized Samsa son my own child
my own dog, along with the five assassinated cats that were
flung dead into our Clos-Salembier garden one with its throat
slit, another crushed, each assassinated by our assailants, all
former dead treated unjustly during their brief lives and still
unjustly since their retreat, like all the improperly buried, the
Ancient Greeks knew a thing or two about that.

I have "on my conscience" as they say, I say to myself, the
strange imponderable weight, the ghostly weight of these improperlyburied, *my improperlyburied*, whom I can neither recall nor forget, their bodies, their cadavers, their identities
forever indefinable, I sense them over there in the corner, in a

14

heap, tangled up in the repulsion I feel first for them and then, on the rebound, for myself, wretched subjects of larval destinies condemned in the first instance to an aborted life, in the second to a death that is a failure, without shape, missing,

the idea of sacrifice haunts me I thought darkly, I am out walking with my brother, slowly and without anguish forty years after the disappearance and destruction of the Clos-Salembier, and my mouth fills with bloody sentences clanking chains from my brother's mouth emerge the howls of madmen he used to hear butchering the psychiatric air, it was on an island reserved for the demented locking-up of the crazed, but nothing on this gentle path foretells pain cruelty desertion, and yet the blood flows, across my eyes flicker intolerable sights I remember not just my own decapitated, but Stendhal's as well, the tortured in Montaigne cruelly add themselves to mine, and to those that flicker across my brother's eyes but none of us is ever at the same place in the scene, we don't taste the same pain, but in the crystalline salt air we hear the same cries. I hear the cries of my mongoloid son, I hear my son's gentle unassuming cries, I hear the Samsa son's groans I hear the crying out of tortured cats in the street and right after that the frightful cadavers come flying through the air and land with a thud on the earth of the garden

I hear the memory of the howls I squeezed out, out of my body, that I drove from my mental vault, in May 1965, a whole day I vomited litters of steaming pigs, monsters, not pigs at all, the horrible incarnations of foreign demons that had moved in with me and occupied my head for months.

I know those howls:

the howls of the betrayed, Siegfried, Samson, the howls of eyes put out

Blindness put out
The betrayed howls with horror
Horrific hymn
In his own psyche
Betrayal squats
One is one's own betrayer
The soul vomits itself up howling

—the day my friend left me I had an upset tummy says my mother. Once I spit it up I was fine.

At which point I catch a glimpse of something over there in the thin reeds lying on the pinched roadway that constricts toward *the thing*: some remains.

What's that? keeping close to my brother. I could see it clearly, the inert vestige, the old rag, but piteous as the body left by a dead child, it's the rest of my Tale, the one I called *The Tale*, what's left of it. Poor bird body left by a bird. I'd fled from The Tale for over thirty years and who knows what messianic impulse had suddenly persuaded me in the month of January—as I'd noted—that what I had never been able to begin to do by myself I was going to do.

"Monday April 2, 2001, antipathy for the word Sacrifice awoke me, the word sacrifice turns up every morning, it's the first one on the paper at seven, fiesta in the living world, the birds warble their celebration joining the chorus one after another and signing their presence in the notebook of the world with a note or two on this day, a model of respect and joy which we, the nonbirds, the restless humans, haven't the nervous systems to follow at seven a.m. in the notebook of the world peace is signed by the birds, but the word Sacrifice bounces off my pen, sticky with blood crawling with vermin. By dint of listening to it

scrape its funereal wings over my flint, I hear it, and I note its notes. Ah! it cries: son!—Ça crie: fils! Sacrifice!—You took your time I tell myself. And I bowed to the impressive Forces that lead us on: the force of deafness, voluntary, the force of refusal, involuntary, the force of flight, involuntary, and the force of the Secret, which is patience without end, total resistance to time. No way to dislodge it. It plays dead. But it's a false dead: no decomposition. It lives outside us within us dies without deteriorating for decades. Immobile, it directs the whole of our play and we know nothing of it. It is the reason for all our choices ands non-choices, the cause of our follies, author of our errors and discoveries."

The evening of Certes I noted: "on the most peaceful road in the world at low tide at noon on Easter Day we were all that was left in the painting, the pair of us, holding onto one another, the posthumous human being." I noted: "in the midst of the peace, on the old tow path, beside us a long hibernation of boats in their sleep, my brother, haunted. Me too haunted. In appearance two blissful passers-by. Invisible a train of monsters risen from the pasts; the haunting, the most shared thing." Two eternally damned. I was thinking beside my brother but didn't say it. One pursued by the father. The other by the son. Clutching one another and pursued, I didn't say it, for fear of rending the illusion of peace in which my brother's shoulders seemed to have wrapped me. I should say: one self-pursued by the father, the other by the son.

At the moment when jotting that down I saw the scene clearly, interpreted by its living characters full of death, reluctant deaths, ghosts visible and disguised, some wearing other masks, the word *sacrifice* came to my hand like the key to this outing.

So this is what it is about: Sacrifice. Suddenly I was handed the word I was hunting for, I no longer hunted for it, I saw a fly alight on my hand each time I think of reciting my lesson, I shake it off with hate, now I see the fly and suddenly I adopt it, I love it, I consider it, separately

According to my brother, my brother has pulled off a one-of-its-kind escape, he was imprisoned in a hetero-imprisonment that for twenty years he'd taken for freely-chosen self-imprisonment, he believed he'd decided of his own free will to become a doctor right up to the day when inadvertently and fatefully leaning a little heavily on the wall of his office he'd produced an infinitesimal and sufficient crack. All of a sudden he saw inside himself, he saw himself from the outside incarcerated without knowing it in the medical cavern to which my doctor–father and not he himself had assigned him, ordaining him sacerdoctor, in a flash the way certain sick people go blind, an extinction so rapid they are catapulted from one world to another *without having had the time* to grasp what was happening to them, he on the contrary had received the intolerable vision of his displacement and even more horribly of his virtually originary and fated deportation, he *saw* himself being not in his place, or more exactly he saw himself in the place he and the whole family had always believed his and having no other place in the world than the one he'd always considered his and he in it legitimately and by choice whereas all along it was just the contrary. Suddenly he'd seen a fool, this fool, the fool, he'd *seen* a lab coat on the fool and the stethoscope around his neck that was really his own broad neck broadened by the years and the coat his own lab coat with one button missing.

By means of an unbelievably painful crumpling of the retina, in a shower of white sparks he saw himself *cast* in a role.

Honest as he is cast as doctor by his father and therefore passionately a doctor, victim of his own honesty, for never before had it occurred to him right up to the moment before "the present hour " that he was only for ever one-in-the-place-of. Is there anything more terrifying than to believe oneself and therefore to be a doctor, passionate, utterly honest without ever suspecting the falseness of the truth?

One spends one's life auscultating the sounds of other peoples' organisms: deaf to the murmurs of one's own heart. Suddenly I saw myself, stethoscope around my neck, incarcerated in the medical office, everything basted together, and never had I seen myself as captive doctor, passionate, chained, a striking look-alike for poor Fips, poor dogs, my brother would say my two dogs I was thinking, my two darling dogs chained at the back of the Clos-Salembier, both doctors of my soul both innocent companions of my secret follies.

All of a sudden on Certes' gravelly white path where I matched my stride to my brother's slow stride as if in a region invented for the timeless time of a dream above which drifted a very bright and youthful sky, in this unwrinkled and dateless landscape without monument, cut and pasted like a slip of paper, I felt the first steps of a book arriving, so neutral and so docile, off-white with the shimmery margins of endless ponds, two swans is all, jotted off to the right I saw, seeing them together for the first time, the two chains in whose absence we were never the two children and the three dogs yapping behind the bars of the Clos-Salembier, where I used to walk barefoot with my brother on the gravelly red path which was already later, which was alreadylater. I shall write I told myself I tell myself fifty years later it was fifty years earlier.

Make a note here: between the times of the place called *Certes* for me, Certes, Certes, I wiggled with my lips and tongue until the word gave way to *Secret*.

Always I've done what I didn't want to do. Therefore I thought I have always given in to the other will, therefore I have always wanted to do what my unwill wanted to do. Every time I had no desire to love I've entered into love with the person I wouldn't have loved. I took the Certes road out of strictness with regard to my resistances. I have always emphatically resisted my resistances. I've stood up to myself and I've won.

Certes really does exist. Certes only exists in reality to lead human beings joined in a dream of movement astray over its whiteness bordered with still mirrors upon which neither sail nor bird. Cluster after cluster of them, by the handful, the long climb or descent on the white ribbon of a perimeter thirty-five years long from any given point of departure, the ribbon endless obviously, as life seems to be till it comes to an end.

Queried by e-mail my friend who exists and resides in New York today responds: the King's Crown Hotel no longer exists if it ever existed I'm sending you the papers, where you say it was nobody remembers such a Hotel, which is no doubt a sign of the casting aside that goes on in New York City everything disappears overnight, here only brief passages. *Don't drive today with yesterday's map.* Which means: don't write today with yesterday's memory. One cannot write yesterday today. One cannot write yesterday. Am I trying to write today? One cannot write today with yesterday, no point trying. Yesterday doesn't come this far. *Don't drive today crazy with yesterday's map.* Which means: don't drive today crazy by driving This Story as though it were yesterday. I hope All This will reach you in time answers my friend: Yesterday Today This, *Don't Drive*. But I see one cannot write today, nor drive yesterday. Trying to write yesterdaytoday requires more mental effort than I am capable of. The King's Crown Hotel absolutely no longer exists. Yet I was there, I was there, once and for all January 1, 1965, judged, weighed, lost, and found in a way impossible to forget, and I'm not the only one. There is no yesterday in New York City there was also a used bookstore which kept every never-yet-read book safe, which has no more yesterdaytoday.

—"I am headed-for-the-worst." Cowardice put these words in my mouth when my brother asked what my next book was about, neither lie nor avowal, not even antonomasia. I didn't dare tell him: G., *madness* G., descent, suicide in G. I didn't dare hear myself say the words, the names. For fear of running away before I set out, for fear the ghost might faint away, for fear my brother, for fear my mother, for fear my pen, my spear, my fork. Nonetheless it's a step. Though not yet the first. Its shadow. I could have said: I'm off to do battle with my cowardice confront what has always made me turn tail before I have time to know who, what, terrorizes me. It's unknown. All around insurmountable Vertigo looms up.

It would suffice to have cleared the Vertiginous Obstacle.

THE EYE-PATCH

Hence the "hidden eye."

On April 6, 2001, the eye thing flashes back again exactly as I saw it on January 1, 1965. This was in the room on the top floor of the King's Crown Hotel where I turned up in fear and trembling, almost devoid as I was of hope, sure I'd never make it, the plane in which I'd been holding my life's breath until it touched down in New York not having touched down in New York but been swept off in the night of a snowstorm until it let itself drop all but broken on Boston. From fogbank to fogbank I descended the floors of hope as the Greyhound bus, I no longer know how I happened to be on it, poked along slow as bad luck, utterly noiselessly and aimlessly wending its way between two cities that were betraying me or that I was betraying between two names.

For now I'm calling this book *The Tale*. The story that The Tale should tell could be contained in two words: *literary madness* or more precisely bound up in a single one: literary-madness. The events occupied less than a year but from this year decades have flowed. The story could be summed up. It's a case of literary contagion. There are only two characters, around whom the others, fifty or so, all thriving, are to be considered as the figures of shadows.

The Tale won't let itself be pushed around.

It is somber, extravagant. *If* you can read, its clear eyes show madness, without trace of a veil. Madness lies in the absence of veil. I mean madness literally. In 1964 I didn't know how to read.

I had *totally forgotten* the *ungeheuer* detail of the *eye-patch,* it was my mother who recalled it just this week, stigmatizing my half-blindness and a half, which just goes to show with what perseverance I go on burying this story even as I try to close in on it. Digging under or digging up? I can't tell.

However on January 1, 1965, I saw it with my own eyes, the renowned eye-patch. I believe the invisible eye the little black patch had replaced was the left one. But there were so many mirrors it might have been right one I can't swear to it,

I've never forgotten, however, nor shall I the scar on the chest I've never set eyes on, true, but which I truly believed I'd seen in the raw. Believedsee.

Today, April 6, 2001, I start a little notebook called *Sudden Returns.*

In it I shall note the totally unheralded upsurge of totally forgotten details. Details dramatic in their day but borne away by time never to reappear, without sequel in my story

unlike others such as the detail of the "half-buried squirrel" whose trail you can follow and me too through almost all of my texts, either in the form of direct inscription, or in the form of allegory or metaphor, unlike the uneffaced, long internalized details, fetishes in no way idolatrized, but recurring, familiar, inseparable those details that have found their way not into my books but into the most inert oblivion, which haven't produced dreams, have had no discernable offspring,

have, however, from the bottomless vault where images and repudiated events repose in a grotesque and macabre pell-mell, the common grave of forgetmemory,

have, however, without our knowledge, without my ever being aware of it not even in those nanoseconds of my existence when, breaking the crust of oblivion, they have shot up and branched out at the surface, where they have gravely injured me, without however giving me a speck of warning

have, however, years later I receive proof of it, traversed my existence, my story, without my knowledge.

First up from the depths and with one lash of its tail to the surface of me, the ultimate, the "eye-patch" detail

the thing, the thing itself, has a name I don't know. I ring my brother this instant, since it is a medical prosthesis his medical knowledge must respond. What do you call I say that thing Dayan like G. wore over one eye?—A patch says my brother, call it a patch for now. All you need to do is ask: the name hides—Think I say—when I know I'll tell you—I need it right now I say.

Yet I went back and forth in front of Eye-Patch any number of times without noticing it, I must have had my head down not to see it as I did on January 1, 1965, in reality; but the head I must have kept down without me seeing me doing this is the head of my memory, my clear and distinct head had probably dozed off from some real or psychic anesthesia. I crossed the same room several times as if it were a Lethe, fortunately, this abolition of consciousness probably accounts for the luck of my survival, better not to see yourself several times I've thought I'd lost an eye in reality as in dream, without ever noticing the dayless night of January 1, 1965 redeploying its curtain across the nights I thought I'd lived through the first time for once and for all. These Nights so fraught with menace, with howling winds I didn't hear, frightened me so that clutching my pen— whose help I didn't have back in 1965—I wrote everything down in order to exorcise it. And even as I noted those very attacks, I saw nothing recognized nothing

—An "eye-covering," says my brother.

G., that is, he whom I have always called Gregor, I couldn't call him, between two Cities, and no phone, the line cut on this side or that, I could imagine his state, I thought I was putting myself in his shoes, the bus poking along in a snowy nightmare in his shoes I saw him, or so I thought, lurch out of the hospital slip into a nightmare of a taxi right to the Hotel where he had decided to wait for me in order to resume the life story, if only for a single day, in the very spot where it had been cut off three months before.

When it comes down to it the only name of a place or person that has ever had a real legitimate and verified-with-my-own-eyes existence is that of the King's Crown Hotel. My friend tells me it has vanished without a trace. The 1965 phone books have been pulped. The inhabitants of 47th Street are new inventions. In 1964 I spent some weeks in this real scenery. All the other names of people, streets, places, addresses, are fictional, the people avenues streets places as well perhaps, beginning with G. But don't ask me. The story remains true, I am proof of it.

I might have had the same love-in-anguish for a different man, for another man without a doubt, this is what I think today, without the anguish and its cruelly subtle and deceptive instruments of torture I would not have loved G., another man completely, different in every way or a woman maybe, but presenting the same over-determined signs to my imagination I don't doubt I'd have had to direct my love-in-anguish toward that stranger especially in those days when, from a point of view that didn't then exist physiologically, I can say this now, without my being aware of it I suffered a relapse.

It would have sufficed that a single detail necessary to the composition of the philter not be there. I would no doubt have escaped the love-in-anguish.

But everything fit, and I found myself on the road at the same time and place as Chance in all his terrible glory found himself on the same road.

This includes the vastest and in appearance least predestined element (study voyage to the USA thanks to a Fulbright fellowship) to the most insignificant, infinitesimal, least apparently spectacular element (speck of dust in the eye of one of the characters).

A pyre of explosives, bombs left underground by the world war, cadavers still too fresh to have changed into pearls and dust, you can live a good while without fretting without a hint of the promise of death in the garden. But one spark at the wrong moment—and this spark is the spurt of tears brought on by the speck of dust in my eye (hence the left, the one with a contact lens). I happened to be sitting across from G. in the necropolitan Library, where it just so happens I had been working for several days, and G. a stranger still about whom I knew only that he knew *Samson Agonistes*, which I had never read a word of, by heart, had just happened to ask me a rather personal question. At that moment a speck of dust slips under the glass of the lens. I felt a searing and familiar pain. I wept. I should have taken out the lens.

* * *

This whole story turns on an eye, now one of the eyes of one character, now one of the eyes of the other. This comment is totally extraneous to the story's events. It belongs to the Tale. To the Tale, that is, version 2000.

Before this date a thin sheet of soundproof glass slipped itself between the story's events and the Tale. So long as I wore a contact lens (that is, *one* lens) I couldn't tell. It was impossible. There was *one* thing I couldn't tell a single soul. I couldn't even tell myself I couldn't tell a single soul. I'd lost the secret, if ever I'd had it, of the telling, of the secret, the thing, the lens. This is something that has never happened to me before. In short you couldn't tell me from this lens. I could no more separate it from my mind than French, I mean the language, of my thought.

I should write that down. But this is still beyond me. I note: now I can say it to myself. But I can't yet write it.

Sometimes I'm tempted to say: here's the Cause. *Die Ursache.* The cause of all these sighings and sufferings, not to be regretted. Everything that happens is due. The cause of the relapse. Although for there to be a relapse, there needs first to be a lapse. The cause of my aberrations of all sorts and degrees: ever-impassioned and passionate errors of love, errors in judging people in whom I have confidence, taking my chosen path to extremes: once you take the first step, straight on to the end, straight on to the end. But such is the nature of love-in-anguish as Freud so often said, and in vain. You don't see yourself take the first step. The cause of all my books, of each one, then the next, and the one after that, of their engendering, in a word all my blinkered attempts at de-blinkering, at dis-enclaving, at dis-anguishing, all bound to fail which doesn't keep you from trying. One small lens. I could write the book of lenses also, an epic of the dreams of lenses and the tragic therefore comic adventures or vice versa comic therefore tragic caused by these magnifying glasses, prisms, *lenses,* glasses: lost in the corner of my eye or dropped and ground to bits, or shattering suddenly into dozens of flakes, or swallowed by the ocular throat stuck in the esophagus, or reduced to a third of their small surface, thereby making sight halting and equivocal, and so forth.

But it is a temptation.

With this magnifying glass you can also set fire to your own bed. This happened to Ingeborg Bachmann, the sole explanation for the fire that was the end of her in 1973. "Disappeared tragically in Rome when the bed in her hotel room went up in flames," says the jacket copy. Disappeared. You can disappear because of what surrounds such a lense, women especially. Nobody warns you. Stendhal tumbled off his horse into ridicule again, but he told us. Proust too stumbled into one destiny instead of another, at least as narrator. As far as Albertine was concerned he was sure that it might not have been her he loved, it might have been someone else. (*Supu—c'eût pu*—he writes in his manuscript in the Bibliothèque nationale.) If only Madame de Stermaria hadn't begged off the evening he was to dine with her, her I mean, he thought. But he would have had to read the letter with his glasses on, to see that the handwriting was not Madame de Stermaria's but the other's, Albertine's. Now for Albertine, to be pursued so, as she believed, after thinking that she had written an utterly unanswerable letter caused her to waver in her refusal to let the narrator love her. Albertine's refusal would have kept the narrator from letting it be her whom he loved. Glasses are the authors of momentous events and of wars just as much as and more insidiously than the eccentricities of people. But once they had eaten together, Albertine becomes the one and only death can put a halt to the enchainment.

In love-in-anguish you really feel that (had you known) you could never have loved the being you-love-forever, all along you feel love threatening you, but you don't know it. The more you feel, the more instinctively you ward it off by increasing the love therefore the anguish.

I was bewitched. Can you talk about being bewitched by a lens? Yes say I. I was bewitched by this lens. I dreamt of it. Through that lens I saw everything, and I saw it askew. Secretly the lens played tricks on me. I was always afraid I would lose it. Furthermore I *did* lose it. I never found it in its place. I walked on eggshells for it might be anywhere. A demon. And it was the apple of my eye. Like a demon it turned me into someone with double visibility. I could see that people didn't see me exactly. I myself looked askance. Let me be talking to someone, the lens got involved, but secretly, it was forever ordering me around and making threats. What if suddenly it took the stage?

A foreign body you take in like an insidious body and indispensable commander of the most indispensable sense, sight. In those days, in thrall to the lens as to an impotent and perverse master, I thought nothing. Everything was locked up tight. Was it faking, what I did? I believe I acted guilty. Objectively speaking, there's nothing wrong with wearing glasses. But nothing is objective. I was doubly flawed vision-wise; on the one hand I saw nothing; on the other hand to this original sin I added the extra lens that was supposed to wipe out the sin.

The Detail makes the Tragedy. No atrocious Tale possible without the frail crack in the wall that surrounds the unspeakable. Othello is contained in a handkerchief. This Handkerchief turns anyone who touches it into a monster. The Detail is this seepage and this handkerchief, which hides-shows, gives on the scene impossible to behold. The Detail is the representative and representation of the act of mutation that turns people like you and me into the monsters of Tales. The Detail is a visual shibboleth, dreadful to behold. Whoever sets eyes on it will never again be the same. Generally, when you enter the Tale for the first time, you pass over the Detail without noticing it. It gets lost among the host of signs. It was only many years later I noticed the Detail that gives us access to "The Metamorphosis" ("Die Verwandlung") though it is perfectly obvious in the entryway where it vegetates and stinks, the eternal cadaver posted as a warning to the reader. But as it doesn't call out or moan or squeak the avid visitor sweeps indifferently past the prophetic vignette and throws himself into the front room from which he doesn't emerge alive. If only you'd read the warning Nothing wouldn't have happened. But by definition the Detail hides what it shows. You *can* always look at the engraving Gregor Samsa cut out and deliberately framed in gilt on page one of the Tale, but it just so happens you still don't see it you never will. The law of Details, how to think of its tricks? It hits you in the eye.

That engraving is a picture of the future.

Why do we always take the roads to madness? But for my mother who goes straight I have always gone zigzag.

Details which take up the whole of the stage, insofar as no matter how vast the landscape all you see is the Detail blown up to the size of the Whole:

—the *Eye-patch* (completely forgotten) which seals off Gregor's eye struck with momentary or permanent blindness during the renowned surgical operation. Gives access to the Darkness of Room 91 and that of the Tale's Camera more generally.

—the *half-squirrel*, a detail which takes up the entire surface of Central Park in my imagination; god of Life-Death. The visible half-body, tail-end of the squirrel, utterly immobile, the breast the arms the head-in-the-ground. *Which side* are we on, life or death, reason or madness, in or out? The question of my life. What if reason were mad?

—The *premonitory engraving* in Gregor Samsa's little human bedroom which shows a lady in a fur cap and fur *boa*, the arm she has stretched toward the viewer disappearing into a thick fur muff

—The *Scar* on G. Hamlet's chest on January 1, 1965, King's Crown Hotel

—The *magic lantern* that projected onto the walls of the narrator's *bedroom*, G.(olo) full of a terrible scheme trotting out of the triangular little forest that blurs the slope of a hill to dark green and spreads out jauntily toward the castle of poor Genevieve de Brabant (who sports a blue sash) with ahead of him a yellow moor the whole scene of this ride slowly moving across the window curtains of the room in Combray, the body of G. himself, of an essence as supernatural as that of his mount

—*Magic lantern* also projecting G. onto the dingy drapes of room 91 in New York (to be continued . . .)

—Are you from Ithaca too? inquires my neighbor on the little plane that bears me from Ithaca to Buffalo. I think about this over the din of the motors. Finally I tell her: yes. I decide vaguely on my American-being. In the end I decide that it is impossible to tell her: I was born in Algeria. In America Algeria doesn't exist. I don't exist. It was less impossible to say I was born in Ithaca. In a way.

Was it because of that Ithaca trip? Soon I found myself confiding the details of my supposed identity to strangers, I never said Algeria, which would have been in vain, but closer more familiar, whatever's most widespread in the world. One must supplement one's identity with the family outbuildings. One person must be composed of one's avowed parents. Have children. How many?—At the moment I say I have two. So small, so far away. Ithaca, O Ithaca *most lost island in the world.*

Not just in the plane. Even in the university Libraries. Even in the Libraries the pieces don't fit.

—Children? asks the young man, my neighbor in the reading room, me Montaigne him Milton.

A YELLOW FOLDER

Went missing in New York in 1965. Then got replaced. But very slowly. For The Tale is just beginning to fall into place.

Innumerable sloughed skins of The Tale from more or less bygone eras repose in *The Yellow Folder*. A file into which I've been tossing vestiges, debris, scraps, hangnails, flakes, prints, chips of defeat for decades.

Stuck to the back of it a flesh-pink post-it. (The color, disposition, shape of the letters, all the concrete details of these notes bespeak surprise, haste, above all the anguish of loss: a state less anxiety-ridden I'd have jotted in a notebook.)

I copy: "E'thing I've <u>forgotten</u>: the roses (or the rose?) in the NY hotel rm (they turn up again in *Angst*)—what good's writing? To forget?"

<u>Forgotten</u> underlined three times, as if forgotten by three forgettings. To which add today the forgetting that followed upon these notes, interrupted for the time being by the finding of the

post-it. Is this the fourth forgetting? How many forgettings does it take to forget, then to forget, then to forget about the forgetting?

I remember the forgotten roses very well, backs straight him sprawled on the couch in room 91 them erect upright legs bunched together in the hotel vase saying we've been waiting for you red long-stemmed, showy, stout, vigorous roses, in the room I don't see them as they are but for what they meant. The room small dark the roses big tall red triumphal pennants upright him lying on the couch. But there.

The post-it is dated: February 21, 1994.

The forgetting has begun again.

I could write a book on Forgetting. It would be about time. I live on big, broad doses of Forgetting. And vice-versa. Forgetting sends away, hides, misplaces, shelters from the light, shakes off.

Forgetting, servant or master?

But I'm way off the track. Deliberately? Let's run this past again:

You see yourself fleeing and close your eyes so you can flee despite yourself. You aren't fleeing, you're fleeing from yourself.

Today I see that not only is The Tale fleeing me, with my help. But that it is its nature to flee because in the year 1964 flight was what it was all about, runaway, fugitive, fleeing flight, swept up in the stormy blast, now real now psychic, such that I see us still, backs bent to the breath of fate or the summer breeze like the passersby caught up in the tornado in a Hokusai engraving, the umbrella inside out, a real umbrella as symbol of the darkness of the soul blown inside-out and obscene in the extra low pressure zone of anxiety's agony.

Crammed into the folder in no particular order, some fifty slips of paper of various sizes, contents, writing styles, of which

(7 April 2001) I sample seven or eight whose ambition was to set foot on that famous American continent of which, as the notes show, I dreamt more often than I can recall, as often, I tell myself, as the great navigators poring for years over misleading though good enough maps, blocked, held back and driven on, abandoning without ever really giving up for once and for all Magellan, Columbus, worn out, as often, I tell myself, as I myself have abandoned without wanting to but suddenly devoid of strength, in a trice: exhausted. Shredded, fell. Suddenly: I was.

↦ List of incipits, stubborn and to no avail:

August 15, 1994. Begin G.'s tale with "The Letter":

1. I was reading this letter the wy. you plunge into an evil wd. –the dream is nt in the brain . . .

it was nt a letter, it was a tunnel . . .

[From the smallness of the writing and telegraphic style, I see I was writing this at top speed in the hopes of getting it down before terror overtook me.]

2. Theme:
—the foreign body
—the stowaway
Planes trains bus then: nothing
Last vision: through the rear window of a yellow cab. Snow.

3. 11.2526.95. Eye scare. Night of the end of the world. Huge terror at the thought of losing an eye . . .

12.17.95 As if I'd attacked the realm of the gods and was being punished feeling myself guilty. At the same time I felt innocent . . . therefore guilty of feeling innocent

12.19.95. Somber feeling: I've been through this before

11.30.95. Gregor is coming back!

Long complicated dream last night: I have a newborn I'd rather forget about, it's up there. The problem is its mongolian unsightliness. But when I go up to look at it I am moved to tears, its animal confidence, behind its debilitating dumbness another sort of intelligence, it twines its arms around me. I say its name *and I weep.*

Tell Gregor's story very simply. But say I didn't live through it like that, But caught up in storms, blizzards, hellish fires, dubious curtains. But say that I haven't lost it—this story. It has become tellable

Dostoyevsky's stories are nothing to this. I've lived through worse.

I was writing a dissertation on Montaigne. The Apology for the Animals. The eloquence of everything. Infinite, sublime communication.

4. *March 1st 1997. Like the first time she "saw" Derrida at the Café Balzar. Similarly when she meets Gregor in the Library. Apocalypses that don't know what they are.*

5. *March 99. The 1999 version? He keeps coming back to this story of folly; each time she tries to tell him the best version the truest. But time goes by and the story changes naturally over time she can't be the same . . . each time you come up with another rationale other clues other ramifications of words*

6. *Undated.*
A terrible, terribly perfect event.
In the beginning I think it seems to me is the arrival-departure of my son George the dead, an extraordinary event that unhinged my life story . . .

7. *April 1994 passing through NY on my own Secret NY—Ny of former days. N'y. Nie: NY. Deny. Deny. History*

*dares not return there—Having taken place in a foreign place
as if in a book in a foreign language. Take The Tale by its Languages you were speaking a new English, countless quotations
of poets in English, I read, he made me read Mandelstam Celan
in English winter1964. A strange foreign English. Scraps of
Russian. Nothing* happened, in French, *as if nothing had happened. Memory foreign a foreigner . . .*

I WILL NOT WRITE THIS BOOK

RETURNS

I stop: at that moment any inborn tendency toward happiness snuffs out. I must not, that is, I cannot write this book, such exhaustion takes hold of me from the very first pages.

But the very moment I write these few lines (still April 6th) my gaze

falls on a wretched notebook page, dated 1998, on which the following phrases—sobs without the rustling of paper—have cast up in choppy, irregular lines:

—*I will not write this book.* [Great white spaces come between the words as if they'd been caught up in the sands of a struggle.]

  —*Why does he come back so*

       often?

 Why   have   I stopped and

written in the place— or—

 Why does he —alwys— show up in the company

   of his 2 figures

my son = the mongolian
and K = the invalid.
He comes back via the fatal illness which is not malady—but
malediction—

Discovered in 2000: the lung at work, undermining my life. Poumon, pou mon *pneuma mine undermined father–Die Lunge. Omi says: die Lunge. K. says: Also die Lunge. I say: die Lunge. Finally I write all around, die Lunge, die Niebe-Lungen—pierced Lung—Siegfried's pneumothorax.*
Poumon: Demon
Dream: remove one of my lungs? Outrged I refuse.
Whereupon confusion in the darkness, I feel as if I'm shut up inside the little lung cage. What if it was Demon? Who to trust?

"I will not write this book." I write this sentence again, date: April 6, 2001, Friday. In 1965 standing at the window of my study where you see what's coming from a long way off. Standing at my study window in 2001 where in 1965 day after day I would watch for the mailman right up to the beginning of April when I gave up watching, having commenced, painfully, to *guess the end.* The Tale: before computers, no fax yet, already tapes. The mailman, same one, same motorbike. Motor. Sputter of letters. That sticky shadow of irritation still comes to me at the time of day when the mailman may have come. This shadow has fallen over my lungs between eleven and twelve every morning since March 1965.

And obsolete the fear of my mother. The Genitive leans now in her direction now in mine. Then the fear oscillates faster and faster and keeps itself in motion. Fear of her fear that is afraid of my fear that is afraid of my mother. It's powerful. The minute she puts a foot on the stairs I put on my detached look.

In 1997—it must have taken some doing to work my courage up to that point, with myself, with her—I ask her what she thinks of the affair, thirty years down the line.—Deplorable! she had said. You still owe me the phone bill.

My interpretive mind spent a good hour all alone with the word deplorable. Had I at that time, in 1997, asked my mother what or whom she meant by deplorable, what would she have told me? My silence gnawed at me. We got no further.

I'm afraid of my mother.

(1) I fear her disapproval:

Still I've never paid the slightest attention to any disapproval manifested at the time of before or after virtually every single gesture and action in the Lives of my brother and me.

I try neither to provoke it, nor with rare exceptions, to avoid it

Maternal disapproval is the salt of my life. Also the stimulant, the pimento, the secret drug.

Without her disapproval I wouldn't have written my books in hiding, I wouldn't have sprinkled the spice of the secret into the circulation of the blood, I wouldn't have buried and kept, I would have forgotten.

(2) It's not her ritual disapproval I fear but something particular in that disapproval aimed at that very part of my life, something toxic, a bitterness and a horror that I myself can taste and that I dread. It's a feeling of committing a great fault, an outrage. She evokes in me a figure so weighty with reproach I am unable to resist. A feeling I am sinning against her maternal soul and consequently against my own maternal soul. As her daughter I have financially sinned and thus behaved as a daughter gravely sinning against her mother and not as a mother responsible woman, by the same token I've sinned against my children whose mother I have shaken to the foundations and betrayed, secretly setting in her place a fearful daughter digging a tunnel under my mother's home. Double matricide and crime against good sense thus against dignity also honor and the taste

for truth, I was in the shadows and the shadows were spreading throughout my entire being.

She fills me with shame, shame wells up, it spreads its strange bitter fire into the thighs into the joints, into the throat, you are sweating. Or is it the debt perhaps? I've always been in my mother's "debt," but that was joyful, debt of birth, of time, of money, of care, of amusement, of discretion, of faithfulness. I am nourished on debts. She reminds me of debts I don't remember, I think she makes them up, these too I accept with joy. I like to keep my mother's generosity alive by digging debts all around her.

I am afraid of her disapproval.

But still-to-owe-her-the-phone-bill is good for me. One part of the Monster-thing is in the keeping of my mother, whom no mad assault can ever shake. I am attached to this debt. I cling to the Branch above the falls. But the Branch scorches my hands.

It is a phone bill, called The Bill, its monstrosity far exceeding that of all the bills in my life unlike any other phone bill no matter how big. And still under my nose.

Or it's a feeling of matricide. Or ill-gotten safety. A wretched, grotesque crime against reality as judge, a desperate act: you throw yourself out the window but slowly for your fall is long, stretching out over weeks and always totally hidden, the window the fall, the reality, and myself hidden from myself under a shawl under the table enacting and re-enacting an utterly treacherous vile and twisted but utterly irresistible fall from grace.

In the story's last weeks, I'd be on the phone to New York for hours every day. Had "the end" not come, my crime would have had a terrifying end, if the bill, having already in a few short weeks turned into The Serial Bill, one and only monster in our accounting archives, had continued to mount, culminating in the bankruptcy of my mother, causing the family's financial and above all emotional and mental ruin, our little ship kept afloat entirely by my mother would have sunk, a crime I might compare to a torpedoing, a chemical weapons attack, all on my head, on my heart, infanticide scenes crowd my mind.

Yet I had but a single idea in my head each day when the time came to phone I followed it the phone and I were body and madness a single thing even today I can feel the rigid and phantomatic incarnation of the instrument coagulate into a plated devil of an animal the minute I set hand on its back, never have I been able to separate from the technical object the satanic illusion it contained when it bound me, me and mine, to the cult of its invocation in New York. If it weren't for the time difference, I think, this fatal episode would have come to its inevitable end much sooner, but at the time naturally I didn't think, I acted, I reached for the phone cries rang out from behind the walls of the fatal room cries rose from the depths of my own kettle of terror till it wore out completely, I took it off the hook I hung up, I horrified myself, everything I did horrified me as well as everything I didn't do.

So much for the money, the bill, here I am on the floor under the table, the devil's tail coiled about my neck, the bill, the money are not on my mind, sense drowns, I'm up to my ankles, up to my breast.

According to my mother, I chalked up sixty thousand francs of debt in other words six million "old" francs. She says chalked up. Intoxicated. Never could I have paid. A debt like that doesn't get paid. I myself could not have paid it. *Had I been able* to pay it this story would never have happened. I had stepped out of the circle of the possible, I could only do the impossible. Sixty million my mother says. A cavern of pus. I have never attempted to close the wound. That sort of Bill can't be erased. Shameful to have let my "folly" sponge off my mother, but without my mother I could not have kept my folly alive on my shame, fraud lies for hours every day. Never could I have bought that for myself except by encouraging my mother to suffer in my stead. I myself wouldn't have done it.

I dug a pit in my mother and threw myself in. In our eyes—mine and my mother's—I was the equivalent of the most wretched of human creatures: gamblers, drug addicts, the bewitched, the deadbeats. I didn't steal: I broke the shell of the earth, I gutted it, I scraped it out. I should have stopped myself but I kept on going right to the end.

I won't write this book, I've decided, I wrote. I will continue not writing it right to the end.

At the moment I *decides*, accepting its weakness, an act in which I recognize my old wisdom—no point in struggling without the help of the body—I promptly consent to defeat, I know when to give in, this is my strength,

the furious strength of the opposite decision rises up in me, a furor I am familiar with, it doesn't admit of any resistance, I've made up my mind, I tell the whole family, I'm the one who gives the orders, to each and all, and the order is an act and a shot of boiling blood, we're leaving tonight, don't unpack, I inform my mother about to settle down, a supernatural or rather natural will resembling that of storms dwells in my heart, my breast my legs I gallop on foot all around the building the past I let go, the dead and the living should just watch out ancestors newborns every one of my selves on the alert I dictate a mental telegram to the fiancé in Asia, this time, I'm sure of it, we're on our way.

* * *

Combat—
At four in the morning the book came
—No no then not that one.

In a few brief hours it tells itself, chant after chant, no no I
was saying, but it always came up with its sentences with age-
old ease.
NY N'Y N'Y va pas
DENY N.Y. Do not go there
It's because of the word *Gramercy*, a word from *Finnegans
Wake*, where I
hushed up
some love notes
Gram Gramme Grammairecy grandmère-ci
Gram Grand Gra-mercy Gra-mare-cy
20th 21 St. Gramercy Park is still closed
I wrote:
I have loved
a *fou* madman
—*lou* wolf
—*mou* weakling
—*tou* all
—*rou* rusty
—*dou* soft
—*cou* neck
—*pou* flea
Each time I go to NY I only go there with: Dread
There are hundreds of important changes you need to know
about.
You need to know y n t k
Hundreds of important changes
You must know

Don't forget
Every day
New York New Yorks York anew

> Night
> March 10, 2001
> I really thought it was him
> this time
> Who had been written

SUDDEN RETURNS

(Little notebook begun April 6, 2001)

—A lock of hair! Among the vestiges, a lock of hair, known as
On the Eve of the Duel with Death, resurfaces.

Later on, in the eighties, I was disagreeably surprised to redis-
cover, in one of those far too numerous boxes brooding on their
volcanoes in the back of my life, into which at variously dated
moments of panic I have tossed a hodgepodge of treasures and
trash that render later excavations forever unbearable, a small,
yellowed envelope without anything written on it, containing a
lock of extremely fine sandy hair. The color. Essence of remorse:
strawberry blond or some such. Was it a lock of my son's hair?
I was aghast at not being able to make up my mind. It's the sole
piece of "evidence," if that's what it was, which I shall never
know, that I have thrown out.

I remembered that his hair was baby-fine.

I write what comes, without explanation.

A lock of hair—is it this one?—snipped on the eve of the day
when, seeing myself about to return to France where my real
children awaited me, I saw him leaving for the unreal hospital
where a battle called *Death's Duel* after a John Donne sermon

48

that I had never read but knew by name was to take place, a battle I took part in afterward mentally, from afar, for three months, conjuring it up in all its details.

In America yesterday I could have been anyone. A hugely terrifying feeling: no sooner had it occurred to me than I became anyone.

A cast-out feeling: foolishly, before taking notes, I'd returned the borrowed book in which I'd just read the summary of my life. Here I am, detached from my self, eyes hanging onto the reflection of me that walks on its side in the tinted glass facades on the other side of 7th Avenue with more self-assurance than I myself have ever been able to muster. On my side, the side on which I get that feeling of being adrift in a foreign country. I suffer from thin skin, my century-old skin my European shelter has failed to fend off the tornado of American Eloquence. The air barks: *The Best Western Inn, The Best Coffee in the World, The Best T-Bone.* What about me? Or is that me side by side with me on the other side? Right away he was *The Best Youngwriter* and right after that on the corner of Lexington and 23rd I discovered he was also *The Best Young Math Adviser* in the pure mathematics division of the Atomic Energy Commission.

A friend tells me: "It's unhealthy to think of the past as real or true. The human being, he says, undergoes a complete transformation every seven years." Still, events remain, even if the Hotel has disappeared or the Hospital was nothing but a make-believe-Hospital everything has occurred for eternity in the imagination which unfolds its map of yesterday, its *American Map,* in the ill-defined vicinity of my today-reality. There are hundreds of *important changes you need to know about* today tells yesterday, but in the meantime today is already yesterday. New York has changed a lot. New York never changes: New

York is in a perpetual state of a-changing. "Every day, road construction crews, State and Federal transportation authorities and local developers are working to make your maps and atlases out of date," *American Map* states. Only in American could you make such an apocalyptic statement. I translate the words but not the tone: *Chaque jour, les equipages de travaux d'aménagement routier, les pouvoirs et autorités des Transports d'État et de l'État Fédéral et les entrepreneurs locaux se liguent pour rendre vos cartes vos plans vos atlas et vos mémoires, nuls et périmés.*

I hear the announcement between NY'*s yesterday* and NY'*s today.* All the transportation authorities local as well as federal are working every day all the time to their heart's content at the variation and mutation of the American language. You can never go back to NY, not even one week later. We are forewarned. The *authorities-other* say: every day we ship off avow disavow dismantle demolish revere knock down show out must submit bar divert threaten fasten dislocate rehabilitate as is proper for American human nature.

The last taxi: yet another Detail. Yet another proof of New York as Shakespeare. In fact everything is metaphor there and perhaps nothing but metaphor. You can't walk down a street without it starting to flash. Somebody knocks at the door: destiny. The days are short of time. In department stores crawling with shoppers I drift from solitude to solitude. In the end with him I always found myself standing outside empty houses built in the nineteenth century and meticulously boarded up. By whom? By their deceased inhabitants? So many empty houses. A general anesthesia. A general amnesthesia. At last the troubling departure day, not knowing who was going where him to the hospital and me to Europe or vice versa the hospital spread all over Europe, Europe was pale weak and NY medical in the complicated Manhattan street we hastened toward a big fatal taxi, the armies camp at opposite ends of the stage and by night the thought of death unites the enemy souls. Tomorrow will cure us to death each thinks of his age for the end is upon us, so soon. Along I went, oppressed, a step away from him feeling the end approach there are so many ends one after another, starting with the end of this empty day in which the Hotel shuts its crown of eyes behind us the taxi was heavy low thick full of itself I tried to slip into it through the left door it was yellow metallic but limping, we saw it had only three wheels, on the rim of the fourth wheel bobbed a little balloon, proof that this scene was happening in reality just like a nightmare, therefore in New York only City in the world where you can drive around in a three-wheeled cab, so full of itself with fake leather and (plastic) stuff that I couldn't squeeze in I still had one leg hanging out when prodded by my long anguish, fearing time was up, I blurted: how unlucky you are! but hardly had I uttered this phrase than it terrified me I wished I hadn't let it go in the taxi that bore us away tacking down the highway he gazed at me brokenheartedly me brokenhearted and so full of reproach as of myself, yes, it's no kind of a life nor leave-taking this lack of equilibrium, this choked-up-with-sentences-feeling, the cab scudded along, so crammed with leather and stuff that even in the cab we were apart I gazed at him, overwhelmed with self-reproach, one leg half out, such a shame.

THE EVIDENCE

—*I'm describing circles around Certes I see myself*

—*You are looking for detours, you are looking for me says the Book*

—*I don't want to find you I say, that's all I dream of, of fleeing you, and this for years and years, I never stop starting to flee you all over again, I describe circles around your circles, detours around your detours, every year, every notebook, another try.*

The most frightening I never stop wanting to say, the most frightening won't let itself be said, or taken, or approached, or forgotten. What a lot of time it gobbles up, it devours! Hours, and not the least of them, long hours stretched taut, giant, mixed, half-elephant half-tiger, trampling stubborn, leathery, white paper to extract what, three words. And you confront the obstacle a hundred times you make a run at it, a hundred times you fall back, you give up.

—*Giving up says The Book is my secret weapon. My double-edged blade. If you give up, you give up—I give up I say.*

And it starts all over again. There's no giving up. You can't give up giving up.

I've had it. Take me says The Book. Take abandon. Grab hold of the most frightening. With all my strength I would but I lack some force to enforce my will. In 1991, 93, 94, 96, 97, I wanted to, I've left traces of this wanting all over my note-books, of the falls and being crushed, at various times or all the times I've written the word suicide but this is a word stronger than all the others, that kills whatever it touches or whatever touches it. Beginning with the book, me, my children, my liter-ary works, my mother, my beloved. I've never suffered so many relapses. Here we go again, I thought. Divided, I leap, I fall back cut into two opposite trains of thought.

The most terrifying of all is the dim fear of saying the worst. At that point a sticky curtain comes down over my eyes, my eyelids are stopped up with cobwebs instead of air a slobbery black membrane surrounds my body.

Yet the most terrifying I am convinced I know it

it is so far so old and now this fear once more strangely frightens me, as if I feared not knowing what I know or relaps-ing into the mental darkness of the past; as if I suspected a simple past might take the place of the past perfect in my memory.

The Thing is dead yet the fear lives on.

—It's not the writing I lack, but the courage I tell my daugh-ter—You don't lack courage says my daughter—If not me then it's the writing.

My days go by in a night without doors without corridors without access, it's an ancient City without any entry, every fifteen minutes there's an attempt to take a taxi, to drive for a long time down the spinal cord to go and knock at the ap-pointed address, it really is number 150 150 Mourning Heights where I've never been but to which I've addressed hundreds of letters, here is the door, sheet metal, you go into a dusty yard children from childhood play there, where is the inside, a little door in the back slips away, it dissolves, you do not enter, you take one street, another, the streets don't take you to any harbor, thus dozens of times you drive the night which is the City divides itself up into hundreds of pieces of nights closed up, this City is made of tag ends of time, you imagine a hostile settlement, in vain you try to get some sleep sleeping, it flees from city to City inside the City, it is always New York but sometimes it is Algiers sometimes Paris for a moment it is Prague immediately afterwards Amsterdam, a potpourri, rotten through and through I tell myself for all these neighborhoods are moldy and strangely emptied of people, a moldy museum of once-proud cities I tell myself labyrinths of abscesses, you spot the Manhattan Hotel where you died in 1965, the Hotel has passed on, death too, all these years you never sleep, or rather insomnia is a kind of disbelief, faithless and unbelieving you sleep, you believe you don't sleep in truth insomnia naps in a succession of sleeps spliced into five-minute segments, when will it end, and each nap is endless, you guess that this is hell, it is a state without existence, you aren't awake either, you can neither rest nor return to the waking state, it is awful you are not dead and no way out like a prison sentence. Time flows on repeatedly without space, moments in chains impacted, sedimented in a retort oven: New York, devil's retort.

The roads which flee from me, let's go after them, let's pursue our reasoning right to the dead end of the corridor, go deeper and deeper in until we are surrounded, poor pack of hounds.

There where speech stops, forbidden, let's leap the wall of silence, speak.

—There is no knowledge nor wisdom all we know is error and phantasmagoria, but there are facts and events.

Speak.

Why have I never thrown out "the evidence"? I never set foot in the cellar or attic, I am scared of the cardboard boxes, the crates, the envelopes, the compact allegorical beasts plump as a good-sized crayfish or a longish turtle, belly carapaced in white skull bobbing with telephone antennae, the old delayed-action suitcases which look for all the world like portable coffins, the miniature cake of soap big as a matchbox still ivory white probably still sheathed in its shiny yellowing paper undershirt stamped with the logo of the King's Crown Hotel.

Why have I never tossed out the "evidence" I wonder, I wrote this question down as it occurred to me, I noted the expression "the evidence" and I didn't touch it. This is a question, it's a fact.

Or ought I perhaps to have asked why I had or have *kept* the "evidence"? This is a question which requires careful consideration an analysis to which we must devote ourselves some other time.

To say that I have *kept* is an exaggeration, I haven't saved, protected, that's never crossed my mind.

On the other hand getting rid of it has never crossed my mind either. It's a fact: in the little tunnel-shaped room that we sometimes call cellar, other times attic others archive are a few boxes that contain the remains, vestiges, exhibits, cartons having held bottles of wine in the beginning, containing dreadful secrets in the end. I'm talking about a number of letters, drawings numerous audiotapes dating from the spring of 1965 in addition to some cassettes.

Maybe there are also some objects? Piddling little boxes for which I'd have given ten years of my life, the last ten years?

That the contents of this file are still around is in itself quite something.

Neither hate nor disgust nor fear have suggested their destruction.

At the moment of leaving the Hotel thirty-six years ago did I think that I would never again set eyes on the brightly lit sign whose naïve shape was more neon cake than crown, I wondered, driving past the other one the Gramercy on the October 1997 day I left New York for Chicago? I asked the taxi driver to slow down but through the dirty glass partition, proof-of-New-York, he acted as if the filth and strips of tape had swallowed up my voice or so I imagine. He too had as costume an undershirt tinted sweat. Did the driver of the separation also have a tattoo on his shoulder? You who leave today in yesterday's taxi Washington Heights has not vanished but they have lost their king and their crown. They'd just assassinated Kennedy in Central Park the question of theatrical sacrifices fluttered to our lips accustomed to murmuring Shakespeare.

I LOVED ABOVE ALL LITERATURE

I loved above all literature ever since the death of my father my being had a definition of quite extraordinary precision that kept me and it from anything that was not literature, now this is the life I thought at dawn I would crack open a book by Stendhal and "the light" darted out; "the light" is this sudden, colorless switching on, all inner fire which, in principle, takes place whenever I get close to a sheet of paper book or notebook page, providing the condition of solitude is fulfilled. I open a book, the light is, right away the tongue begins its tale, I'm forever remaking myself with these literary molecules I told myself, then as now, it is six o'clock in the morning maybe seven, I hear the regular and strangely powerful breathing of the books on my shelves. Since the death of my father, they've been breathing like human cats. I was writing a thesis on the note-of-banishment-in-Shakespeare. Thirty-five years ago banishment was unable to play its poignant music except in Shakespeare. I did whatever I liked. I lived where I wanted to. In Stratford, in

London, in Illyria, elsewhere. The note of banishment filled my thoughts with the enchanted music of mourning. Who cared about the rest of the world? I had reading for all time. I had left Paris and its Schools, where they didn't want you says my mother because you were a young divorcee, a pity, says my mother not at all I say luckily they wouldn't have me in the Schools, luckily even before I got in I was banished but right away, in return, I banished Paris, the Schools, in Paris I'd have had to bend my thinking and it would have bounced right back up and smashed everything. Right after my son George's disappearance I took to the roads of literature I kept my distance from cities and schools, and I left to study the theme of banishment, whose music had a familiar ring, in manuscripts conserved in the usa thus safely banished by a process of paradoxical safekeeping. Passionately and reverently, off I went to consult the manuscripts, the radiant remains of the-to-my-eyes holy works, which the Europe of Schools would have none of whereas the voracious American Libraries had clearly longed for these relics fortunately collected and kept on the far shores of banishment where, later on, from the places that had seen the birth of these grains of light you crossed countries and oceans to go and share the miraculous bitterness of the experience of passovering that never ceases to repeat itself, again and again throughout time. I also went to consult the manuscripts of *Ulysses* and of *Finnegans Wake* in their mad diaspora, with tears in my eyes, I was indignant even as I rejoiced at the blind behavior that brings the political organism and the individual organism together. Either the body (political, individual, cultural) is good-natured about its most precious organs, its poets, its artists, its eyes, its dreams, or it is not and it begins to bomb and chase away its kings, its queens, its prophets, till they are fed up, never is it the least bit grateful for the apples of its own eyes.

Feverishly I went after banishment, why did I bore myself to death in schools I tell my brother when I arrived from Africa, on the run, finally I'd escaped Algeria which didn't want me till I no longer wanted Algeria either. I am observing our childhood from the balcony of this house says my brother and I see that you have never ceased chasing after the trace of banishment, look at this house, I would die of boredom here, you have shut yourself up in the outskirts of a city awful to behold in which you never set foot, I see that in the end you have banished yourself to a building that's a lot like a paperback book.—If I'd left Algeria and our childhood of regret and powerlessness it wasn't so I could end up in France, I took the boat as soon as I could in my life so as to put some distance between me and one shore (and not to get to the other shore the very idea of reaching the other shore horrifies me, I never wanted the other shore except lost in advance, except vanishing, as disquieting and fascinating as it was desirable and repellent just like the dream shores of Lake Averno in which the unreal landscape with its veil of sulfurous fumes is merely the hint of imaginary countries) for once and for all I took a ticket for getting away from, not for getting close to and at this I was a big success, the getting away I got it and I never again lost it on a boat I had no port of arrival in view even when I took the giant boat for the USA it certainly wasn't for the USA but for the Library thus secretly for my home base at no permanent address where those whose gift is for banishment are wholly embraced and taken in, the idea of banishment being respected there without being capitalized on, there is no professional banishment, nor is there any enrichment, only a tent roof over the campsite. In the USA I didn't go from city to city but from one Library to the next, and even from one manuscript collection to the next. In my mind I took the boat that was moored between the columns of the British Museum for the monumental Beinecke Library, even if in reality I had to cross cities roads ports oceans ports cities airports roads that went from Paris to London to New York to New Haven to Buffalo. I wasn't about to be separated from the theme of my complicated but meticulously organized trip: I went straight for literature as banishment. I wanted to interview the giants. All I wanted was to spend my life with the giants, no one else only the giants with giant works. I didn't know myself at all and I didn't interest me. I simply loved Literature as Higher Monstrosity. I enthused over corpses changed into pearls *Full fathom five thy father lies, those are pearls that were his eyes* over and over I repeated the magic words and nothing bad could happen. Literature changed the corpse of my father that was all I asked: the sublimation of the corpse I tell my brother is what I was looking for.

I got over the terrible suffering of the cemetery that we shared with a book I say to my brother. I never went back to the cemetery. I would read. I went right past the body on into sentences. I made sentences of my father. I wasn't losing papa any more I say. I wasn't losing any more. I had found the pearl mine. Whoever finds pearls finds pigs as well said my mother, but the pigs I put down to her taste for proverbs. I was possessed: I didn't know it. It never crossed my mind I was losing in another way: I was on the brink of perdition. I didn't see that I didn't see myself. I was losing losing and so high up on the shelves of clouds that I had no alarm system, conscience, presentiment. I was adrift in change. I would read. Everything that could be done with a book in hand I did. Scarcely had I given birth, quick, Montaigne, I would laugh to see the new face of my son, the other one the one after, I no longer thought about the one before, I went on, no turning back, on and on I read and no nostalgia no sooner born than he too is a future reader of my Montaigne who had already read and sketched his newborn portrait foresaying everything the speech of the hands as of the head, and the eyebrows and the shoulders there is no movement that doesn't speak Montaigne I told my newborn son. And there is no creature I read to my infant whom Nature has not provided with everything he needs to survive: shells husks bark hair wool leather underfur feathers scales fleece silk claws teeth horns weapons clothing and just as the elephant grinds and sharpens the teeth it uses in war (having some special ones it keeps for this purpose and never puts to any other use), so to strengthen its mind and body the child has his stock of books. There are books for war and books for peace, books to complain with, others to rejoice, books to call to one another for help, books that bid us to love. Whatever I couldn't do with a book I did fast, without leaving the beloved in my thoughts, and as soon as the child was bathed and dressed, I would go back to my book I laughed at its wit. I couldn't not laugh. For me literature has always been the greatest and most sublime of affairs the only one that makes me laugh in the midst of the torment.

I was sitting at a table in the new Beinecke Library, reading three Ulysses at the same time, Homer's Shakespeare's and Joyce's I went after them in all the languages I feared and admired him I loved his dog who loved him above all but I didn't love his cunning I was laughing to myself and across from me an American reader chortled, whereas coming from Europe my laugh was an intimate thing, over on the other side Milton made him burst out laughing on my side beside Montaigne I smiled.

—Why was I bored to death during my eight years of medical school my brother exclaimed I'm going to tell you, it's because I wasn't doing what I wanted to be doing. It wasn't *my* studies I was studying medicine in place of a dead man who loved doing what I hated and I couldn't even clearly hate what I hated since being a stand-in for a dead man I was a dead man's suffering.

I listened to my brother's words and I found them beautiful, I approved of his phrases, I said them over to myself, I was moved by their charm, thus Telemachus the stand-in must have mulled things over I told myself and no longer was I thinking just about my brother saying how much he had suffered but also about the poetic way in which he expressed his complaint—and me too I say, listen I'm going to tell you: why I tormented and betrayed myself scared to death of being myself the betrayer in the *Gregor affair* (I said the *Gregor affair* now, I used the word Stendhal used to speak of the Julien or the Sorel affair, whichever).

It's because I was allowing myself to be ruled by a dying man who was not in point of fact dying, I was fighting for the survival of a sick person who wasn't sick and the fact that he wasn't really dying or ill which I didn't know gave this reality a supernatural theatricality which overwhelmed me with anguish, whereas if Gregor had really been dying and not just pretending, the scene would have been weaker and no doubt less bewitching. And not one day for eight months did I betray my torment and fear of betraying with which I kept faith, with every ounce of my strength.—Fifty years I've served says my brother, fifty years in the opposition I've served the desires of a dead man with whom I was commanded to identify.—But sometimes I say eightmonths are never-ending sometimes an eight-month leaves on the soul an infectious shadow that you can't efface, nothing but a shadow, but nothing's more powerful and threatening than a shadow. It sleeps and you never know what it is up to in that unexplorable region, draped unmoving mute perpetual without any sign of regression.

64

I too feared betraying an almighty-other (hence as most free people abandon their lives and beings to another-power, some of them even going so far as to make themselves stay at the side of this other power, because of its foreignness and the way in which it vaguely recalls some vanished power, in life as in death, I as a free person had sworn off life and being for an eight-month. But only because death was in the offing I swore now to my brother, but under no condition could I have admitted this to the person in question, he, that is, who appeared to me for the first time on the ramparts of a library, without which I say now to my brother I would never have bothered with him but under no condition could I have admitted this to the Gregor in person) I had sworn body and soul and most religiously to serve him as an army serves its captain. What made a young man my captain is that on the one hand I was the daughter of a dead-captain on the other this abnormally literary character in the role of dying person spoke to my imagination. I too feared betraying one of those fatal presences who govern us with a power inherited from omnipotence-others, for an eight-month and maybe fifty years later still, I have obeyed a ghost quite otherwise ghostly—because forged of unreality—than the real ghost of my father, for the former, Gregor, was merely a temporary and put-up version of a dying person, a fabulous construction-montage of quotations and allusions borrowed from classical and the very last word in world literature.

You never know whom you obey when you act imperiously against your own will.

Of course my father hadn't given any orders to my brother but perhaps my brother had obeyed the pure authority that my father had gone and left in his place I was thinking and therefore nonetheless the absolute figure of my father. We always were disobedient, each of us forever doing as we pleased my mother complains, but if what you please is under orders to another, then you may not be pleasing the person you think are. Perhaps, had my brother wanted to be a doctor, so as to exercise paternal and ghostly authority over himself, he would have refused to be a doctor as adamantly as he'd condemned himself to be one. At exactly the same period I: obeyed. We were forever obeying in spite of ourselves.

I was forced I say by the conjunction of my unconscious hypersensitivity to the premature death of a male being and my violent enthusiasm for literary inhabitants. But naturally not only did I never breathe a word of this but in 1965 I never thought it either. I'd never read a line by Freud, but Dostoyevsky, The Devils, never left me, get thee hence, I told myself as my heart devoured the blood and gore of Stavrogin the love-of-murder that does itself in.

1. I caught sight of him and what's more without seeing him in the Library, rare manuscripts room

2. He was laughing out loud reading Milton

3. He coughed a little but I paid no attention, careful not to let it get on my nerves

4. During the day I no longer remember at what point we were drinking coffee on a bench, I responded short and snappy all my time being for books

With his first book forthcoming in December 1964 from Knopf in New York he was the young writer who was going to change the course of American literature. Never mind Faulkner. Since Poe. Since Melville. The great phantom-theme of the haunting without which there is no literature was about to resurface.

I hadn't the least desire to write I was a fervent reader the books I might have needed to write having been written it remained for me to read them unlike anyone else, I had become a hunter of exceptional skill subtlety and perspicacity. With *Death's Duel* the young man would give American literature back what it had inherited from European literature, but cast aside in order to take the new roads with no memory. Donne Pascal Milton he was one of them but now he was sprinkling the metaphysical poetry of the new testamenters with a dash of Jewish spice suddenly he was striding up and down in front of the bench outside the library and introducing me with a chuckle to his totally-unknown-to-me Jewish cousins and second-cousins, head thrown back, in a trance, voice husky, he tossed off incredibly bitter but poetic accusations or vice versa so poetic so bitter, he proffered them like stones in the face of the American sky I was stunned by the state of sad jubilation that swept over him

I gazed at him with the self-assurance and serenity of someone who does not fear being hypnotized by the hypnotized

but it was a Mandelstam poem I'd never heard of that so stirred him up and which he was acting with such genius that I would have been hard put to differentiate between creation and interpretation, besides I believed such complete reinvention-reincarnation was impossible, to this day I ask myself if this poem was not however by him then who was that utterly possessed person?

I gazed at him with the severity meant to keep people in danger of being hypnotized out of harm's way. *I*, I told myself, am not the sort of person to let myself be taken in by an attempt at charm.

I no longer recall the poem but I recall the poetic state and I saw no difference between the two. Head thrown back like a rooster about to chant its broken song, mask honed, hair already sparse on his brow, voice low, warm, breaking, and then he coughed.

I gave a little cry and jumped up feeling I had perhaps been hypnotized. I gave a little cry and I gazed at him with the falsely natural look of one who has just been stung by a bee.

He had reached the secret of music, a hoarse rattle, and to say that a little worm sups on the heart and life of a great poet he says to me, sitting down and shattering my daydream with this sudden about-face.

I gazed at him with the mingled self-confidence and uneasiness of someone convinced she is unreadable going bald, the look of another age already, voice singing and sad, one of those basses you sometimes hear caressing themselves in a little synagogue, and each of his poems is like a stone deposited on the century's tomb. It's him to a *T* I said to myself he was talking about Mandelstam his father had known him it's a self-portrait I was thinking, he was extraordinarily gifted he was saying, I was thinking, at such interpretation-evocation acts.

I didn't look at him.

I was struck by an onomastic resemblance between his name and that of my son the dead but I promptly pushed aside this semblance of a resemblance, what could be further removed phonetically from George than Gregor, at which point he drew my attention to the anagram saying that up till now they'd been called George from father to son in the family, meaning his, and that he'd come along to cut the cord. I am *the one who sees to* the cutting of the cord he said. He was missing a tooth up top on one side, you hardly noticed it. *Gregor?*

I must have looked at him. With what trembling self-assurance remains to orphaned mothers who pretend not to fear the ground swell of regret, I thought of my son whose name is of the earth whose disappearance is still very close and already so distant. Then right away I ceased turning back, I got up, I headed for the Library.

This face was now dispossessed. Absent-mindedly I looked at it and without my noticing it I noticed how little there was in it now worth noticing.

THE NECROPOLIS

"Like those with but a few months left to live. Like those with but a few months—how young they are." He was saying. "That's how I speak to you: like those with only a few months left to them."

What was that supposed to mean? I read the sentence two ways: (1) those who have only a few months left to live save time, thus avoid detours, unnecessary frills, expressions of courtesy, segmented syntax, hypotaxis. They cut short, they go straight. Style sober naked plain and at the same time equivocal, amphibological. Brief. (2) and conversely: having all the time in the world they therefore use it with drunken prodigality, stay on the air for hours, waste yours, which is limited, in endless blather and long monologues.

In both cases a kind of obscenity develops.

I found the expression disagreeable. I found this comparison sickening. Presumptuous I tell myself. Right away I choose not to attach any importance to such pretension, excessive, I tell myself, suggested perhaps by the presence on the shelves of the great Beinecke Library of a great many books written by the famous and admired or admirable authors who really and truly had only a few months left to live everybody of course is moved by the fate of Proust, that the reader should feel a conscious or unconscious jealousy for this last heat is a normal sort of naïveté, so long as you yourself don't have a whistling, wheezy lung you can be consumed by romantic envy, in the end the reader is always dreaming that he is the author in every respect starting with his shortness of breath; still you mustn't flaunt your envy. I thought his declaration unwholesome and unseemly. All the more so in a Library which is in so many ways like a Necropolis, this Beinecke where untold volumes testify to illness and deathbeds. As we young readers with our paper, felt-tipped pens, cups of coffee, were busy reading and leafing through books, and me, the still warm manuscripts of those always prematurely dead authors who've vanished and taken with them the eternal nothingness of the hundreds of books they didn't write, didn't finish writing, hadn't thought of before they went and whose faces and names we'll never know. So many missing books. But not death which I personally never gave a thought to, the works having neither age nor death and only the works eternally and youthfully bright, and their births interest me, I thought, deliciously leafing.

He had said the indecent words with the smile of an old man. With a grimace, I pushed away the words, tasteless on the young lips of a reader with his female skin, seated with nonchalance and coffee as if representing to himself—craftily and perhaps in order to gauge my sensitivity or competence in the matter of tropes—some sort of team. Later on, moreover, I had a strange feeling that on the phantasmic diurnal scene he could, at will, produce the effects of zeugma, at any given moment he could yoke abstract to concrete in his speech as in his representations of himself. Zeugma: one may not know this word with its ring of eloquence and being sensitive—all the more sensitive as you are not familiar with its hidden spring—with its outrageous and preposterous effect. I didn't know the concept, only later on was I to discover how calculating Gregor could be, right to his rhetoric so well cloaked by his aura of weird spontaneity. Coffee is my nonchalance he signified. Turning up in a pair of white jeans, he would say I'm so harassed.

The jealous young reader dressed in gray in old but tidy shoes, not in sneakers, envier of lung diseases to the point of coughing a little whereas the lung does not a genius make I was thinking. Like a discrete and reserved visitor, that's how the reader should behave, and not tarry overmuch in the Library.

The reader locked up for months with the works and sometimes the manuscripts of beloved authors suffering from incurable illnesses ends up confusing the work the sick man and the disease the work as disease the disease as work the disease as author, the Library as transfigured Hospital. The reader enters the work via the disease, enters the disease as into a precious neurosis, tuberculosis is now his one and only love, he reads Keats for Koch, no longer can he wish or hope for the author's cure for this would be tantamount to choking off his genius. In the Library he heads for where the books cough. Inside the Beinecke what's more is cruelly like a brand new hospital room. It reeks of sterilization. I entered the great Yale University Library as into one of those great halls where the hospital adversary waits to pounce the minute I enter the Beinecke I'm in a hospital I remember I thought embarrassed and ill at ease was it because of the way the windows were disposed, the shadows meant to be welcoming for a fleeting moment I believed and feared I'd glimpsed my father in them cut off from the world of the living by a vast and luxurious pane of glass, I enter the Beinecke right away a mirage of Mustapha Hospital comes to meet me, the images of the dead who are part of us and have departed from us do not die and they start flashing whenever a setting lends itself, so the Beinecke reminded me of my father's last days and that moment when not yet dead already he wasn't on the same side of life as me and was drifting off without moving like a ship in a dream. Already fifteen years I told myself quick yesterday is fifteen years old already and I was frightened by the thickness of the volume of years that stretched between him and me, whereas today it's fifty-three years and still yesterday I tell myself but from a distance of fifteen years you are still right up close to the fatal scene. All the more so as it had been replicated though less intensely, but the replica sets the shock waves off all over again, for George, my son, had also disappeared behind the soundproof glass and this just two years before the Beinecke.

But since you can't read flanked with coffins I only caught glimpses of one or the other of their ghostly phantasms—with my eyes I saw them, as on a faded, animated photo, fragment of old film—bare outlines with that vague clarity typical of double exposures, sitting alongside a row of big volumes, I fluttered my eyelashes to chase their dusty faces from my eyes, and in a twinkling: exorcised.

So it got on my nerves to hear this youngster toying with the idea of premature death as he blew on his coffee.

The Beinecke may be thought of as the phantasmagoric pyramidal tomb of many prematurely reaped beings. I have always detested and feared libraries. Each evening white-coated librarians ought to scare away the readers who want to stay and spend the night in the rooms full of eternity reserved for those who have become ill-read but envied gods, humble former writers,

74

anguished, hard-working, raised though too late for them to the altars of the bookshelves.

At lunchtime I stepped from the glorious cold into the sheet of August sun. Sitting on a bench I made fast work of my home-made European sandwich, but not too fast because of the squirrels. I felt comfortable with the squirrels. I speak their language. Today as thirty-five years ago I commune naturally with the black Canadian squirrels, with the big gray inquisitive American ones, with the rusty-colored black-plumed cat-bellied squirrels of my garden. Living gods totally innocent of death and of life as death is what they have meant to me ever since squirrel-the-first, Central Park Squirrel, half interred, whose transfigured portrait I came across in the Prado as Goya painted it according to his own anxious nature. Saved by the squirrels who know neither mourning nor banishment nor up from down and who are modern-day phoenixes, sole creatures capable of re-birth in the five minutes following the exhalation of their last breath. And at the same place-moment on the bench, shaken out of my dream of consolation by the intruder, at the very moment, on the bench, when the hostage of the Necropolis be-lieves she's escaped

along comes a black sentence up out of the darkness, smil-ingly exhaled, turning up as if from the eleventh book of *The Odyssey* from the depths of Erebus.

The rest of the University was surely gothic I don't recall, imitation gothic, American scare-baby, far more impressive in its make-believe than European gothic, and without the slight-est possible link to the Algerian coastline where my rivers have their source, I was never able, once I'd debarked, to find the passage, either as if I myself were a shade searching for a way back to the side of the light or as if the scenery were that of the shadow-land and I inhabitant of Light trying to accustom myself to this other world for the time being. The ancient-modern marbles of the Beinecke, the livid whiteness, as if the idea of past had stolen in to mix with the blueprints of the famous contemporary architect according to the macabre method Poe describes for the decoration of Ligeia's unconscious dwelling in "Ligeia."

I wrote that in April 2001 after having first come across that picture again, the one that looks like "Rouen Cathedral. Saint-Romain tower and portal in the sun" but as if stiffened sealed in the amber of the most distant memory, but still with those shining pale and blue hues, then the name of the Necropolis that I first called Meinecke then finally Beinecke.

That's where my Tale should begin, in that Mausoleum for a Tear.

I wrote with my eyes riveted to the picture painted in strong contrasts of light and shade at whose foot I see myself in a garish orange dress, to be taken as the character's costume for this first act, when I had as yet to be caught in the soft ultra-strong net of the pneumonia which to my stupefaction laid me low on the very day when, like the falcon freed in the Egyptian Book of the Dead, I was about to fly off to my writing perch and which to this day remains taut repetitive impassive unshakable stretched across my life like one of those cyclonic phenomena that to the astonishment of the inhabitants of our new millennium settle in forever apparently over the shores of a continent, and brood and brood until modern nations feel the Neolithic generations' archaic beliefs in the superior powers of evil astir in the depths of their thoughts.

The sky: unmoving, empty, in 1964.

I wrote that in April 2001 without any accompaniment on the part of my lungs, with jubilation and deep breathing or inspiration, perhaps the feeling of having after thirty years of searching underground found the shaft that ushers you back up to the light.

Thirty years ago I thought nothing. But I was *inside* the Beinecke where I felt an inexplicable uneasiness, I had only one peripheral idea: be done as quickly as possible with consulting the manuscripts to which I had allotted ten days so as to be able to leave and at the same time flee the superb building that weighed on my forehead and breast as if its marble torso had collapsed onto my body.

I have forgotten where I was staying nothing is left of the neighborhood and its surroundings. The marble mountain still crushes my heart. This summer, awakened, if dead giants can wake, it weighs on me sinister grown active again and omnipotent like the print of a tuberculous volcanic formation roused from its cold youth frightening whose whole weight instead of remaining in the outer vault insinuates itself into our real lungs where incomprehensibly it plagues our breathing. As if the lungs impelled by the force of magic images took to imitating the constitution of necropolises.

I am convinced I shed the famous tear, the true-false tear, inside the Library. And for this tear, as a result of this tear, fate took a turn it is hard to credit. But all turns have in common the slightness of the occasion, a slightness that is the essence of tragedy. And all tragedies have for cause and emblem the infinitesimal, derisory, terribly small deposit of an element that weighs next to nothing, a leaf on the shoulder, a slip of the tongue, a tear, a moment's hesitation.

Because of this tear an impassible barrier became passible. The man reached toward my hand, an unacceptable gesture, rendered permissible by the tear interpreted as having been brought on by a sudden access of grief, whereas it was in fact caused by a stabbing pain in my cornea. Anyone who wears contact lenses knows all about such sharp and unbearable pain.

This little pain is not only sudden and sharp but generally completely ill-timed. It gets you in the eye while you are up on some social stage. Either you exit right in the middle of the scene of your lecture to flush out the lens under which a speck of dust has slipped, or you weep outright. The audience is free to read these tears.

One should not weep: no tear but splits in two as, abashed, it runs down the cheek on the side of the nose. One would like to stop it weeping: tear disavowed. One can't tell oneself what to do: of oneself one does not approve. I didn't cry: a tear escaped me. To some it resembled the tear of a grief-stricken mother. For that Beinecke self of mine not even half mine—a self I can barely reconstitute so many years later, whom I have trouble admitting to whom I mean to admit, there on the Beinecke bench—it was a defensive tear, shed on her own account, to help her out, shed over her awkwardly ruseful, addressless self.

She could go wrong, sin for a lens.

Nor is there, however, any savagely egoistical tear that does not contain a drop of regret.

The man extends his hand in sympathy. And that was all it took to seal up. for decades, the trace of an original sin.

It is all the fault of a tear stolen from the recently dead child, in vain do I attempt to describe the sacrilege, then the shame began, the small betrayal of the most delicate part of oneself.

Where to place intimacy? To the foreigner it felt less wanton to let the voiceless and faceless silhouette of a child dead not long before the Necropolis peek out than to reveal a bathroom secret involving a highly sensitive part of the body. She held the lifeless body of her son up in front of her face like a shield. Mask of the deep-down mask. That's when the man touched her hand and she withdrew her hand.

Already at the Beinecke he would utter sentences that began with "Man": "Man is time's mishap." "Man suffers from the slowness of time except when he is suffering from the quickness of time." "A man without a past has no future."

How can you say sentences beginning with man at his age or ever even?—How old are you?—25:52. It all depends. She who'd never have begun with man.

I thought I was lying in telling a lie, in choosing to say that I was weeping, it is so conventional, as a young mother recalling the death of my son for whom I had not in reality ever wept, quite the contrary, for his death was not a simple death and it had taken place in a place beyond the staging of tears, I hadn't wept, not for his death either, in reality, I was still far from doing so, I had lied rather than own up to the stabbing pain provoked by a bit of grit scraping my cornea, which had wrung from me a flood of lubricating tears but in lying I had spoken a truth so profoundly buried inside me that it could never have sprung forth save masked as a lie. My mother too, I have since learned, lies in order to tell the truth without its envelope of anxiety. But the lie told the truth, the only way truth can find to make itself heard: to pass itself off as simulacrum. Just as in 1965 I was totally incapable of revealing the presence of a revolutionary foreign body in my left eye so I was incapable of revealing the huge pain of the absence of damp and noisy pain that the death as unbearable loss of my son was causing me. When the insult to life as body and world is too great instead of suffering bodily you are soul-stricken. I had already experienced this with the amputation of my father, this shame of being sectioned, crippled, invalidated. Despite the moments of grace, we had so suffered from life's suffering that in making us inconsolable death gave us a measure of peace and the luminous cruelty of this I was unable to think in 1965 without my head reeling in a fog of confusion. I could not see through the fray of contrary emotions.

G. was trembling too. I'd forgotten about him. I couldn't not forget this naturally repulsive detail naturally. Here he was, him too given to that terrible little shiver that traversed my son's body with the speed of neurons firing. His hand too trembles a little, when he lifts a cigarette to his lips. Could I have seen in that frail plucked creature a ghostly illusion of my son in adult form had he lived? I don't believe so. But it sometimes happens that I feel my thoughts stir as if from the melancholy breathing of a ghost stealing off into the shade of the shades so as not to attract attention, but still allowing a ripple to give him away.

Vain posthumous attempts, pale brotherhood of the dead who are forever trying their luck and for what? Call on one of them and suddenly alerted by a whiff of the thought addressed to that one all the lost and forgotten press at the gate of the chest, fighting over the heart and clamoring to be heard, for in each of the dead all the dead begin their deaths all over again, in one dead all the dead, each for the other. They never sleep except like cats with their ears pricked. Any allusion, the least detail in common, a crossing of two traits among the thousands, immediately, hungrily they leap at the chance to fling themselves toward the living. And vice versa G. living jealous of the death of the dead.

You wonder what entity, what hostile passerby traversing a being so propagates the thousands of nervous twitches. A poison, a morbid obsession, the announcement of mutation? Of mutilation? My son too, tiny being that he was, already knew too much about the human verdict.

—Stay. Two more days. Says he. Or:—Stay. Why don't you stay? This is a rough translation of what he says in English. *Why don't you stay longer?* The problem is that English now having but a single pronoun for the second person you never know if the person who is thou-ing you is not you-ing you the distance between indifference and invasiveness is all too quickly effaced.

—*Stay.*

I refused. Under no circumstances would I have changed my plans in the sixties. We were on the eve of my departure for Buffalo my next library. I got on the plane. We'll write.

"But the letters don't come, the ghosts are eating them," he says and I didn't beware these words. Ghosts live on faith and I hadn't any. Or so I thought. I was haunted without knowing that ghosts were at the commands of my dreams my decisions my rules.

In 1964 I listened to Mozart's *Requiem* hundreds of times, in parts, for whole evenings, voluptuously, believing I listened to music and that was all. I loved the *Requiem* above all and in the *Requiem* the *Dies Irae* I never tired of it I never saw myself not heeding the warning. You can read without reading, I was wrapped up in this withoutreading. Ecstatically I withoutread the rugged hymns of the Erinyes I feasted on the stanzas of Aeschylus as if they were ice cream cones melting on the fire of my tongue. I hummed ferocities deliciously. Nothing else gave me such pleasure. And this is how ghosts steal up singing on their future prey.

And yet I had already been under attack. Twice already the split Earth rolled its open flank in front of me the cosmic carcass bashed in I lived for years ungrounded pushing a rusty perambulator heaped with my discombobulated life ahead of me. But I always went on pushing my life ahead of me.

No longer did I spin dizzily into the giant craters into which had just dropped the petrified body and minuscule stones of my father and shortly afterward of my son who bore the same name as my father and thus the same fate.

I had been terrified. But I had not aged.

I hadn't howled the beastly howls, I hadn't wanted to die in order to cut short the terror.

Each time I'd wanted to live. I'd cracked open a new book.

I got on the plane. I went on pushing my life ahead of me. I did not recognize the copy of the ghosts.

MORE AND MORE NOTEBOOKS

More and more notebooks, I am now writing on a dozen note-books whose dis/superposition on my desk, due to my convul-sive movements, now coming alongside, now nervously pushing off again—(but I don't throw out, I push off) depicts my state of panic—I write in skirmishes. Big notebooks, as against my normal fidelity to small notebooks. In fits and starts followed by brusque abandons. A big broad brand new white notebook seems to evoke the spirit of initiative. But in the end I get lost among these wounded, rejected tablets. At which point I go in search of myself. Recall a page of notes that seems to me to have been, to still be I hope, the one that might survive the hecatomb. I can't find it in the ruins, I dig, one writing day lost scrabbling in upside-down convulsions of convulsions that have dispersed the sheet of paper that I hear, I think, breathing—gasping under the landslide. I scratch, I think I find, all these sheets look alike, all these pale blue notebooks, not-to-find to this point what does that mean I thought, the harder I search

the more I lose, it seems I am burying what I am trying to ex-
hume, "nobody can see me" I tell myself (every now and then I
switch pens as if I absolutely couldn't do without the help of a
stronger or more tenacious pen, furthermore I ought to scratch
out all the as if's because there aren't any, in this state of mind
there is no distance, it is painful, an aching right to the bone,
mental, but to the bone, to the nerve) but "nobody can see me"
my thought thinks, this is not a complaint or a consolation it's
a relief, here I can let myself go in a frenzy of self-bewitchment,
a ferocity of intention well known to the great virtual criminals,
this furthermore is how you know born-scribblers for whom
nothing can put a halt to the crisis of writering (I don't mean
writing, this takes place beforehand in the understory of the
writing, before the appeasement) no intervention or ethical or
police influence, no emergency can pretend to be more urgent
than the frenetic mental nervous urgency of coming to terms,
finding the term for it, often it's a matter of a word, a phrase, a
page, an illumination, a nugget, buried, promised palpitating
that still gasps in the caved-in shaft but risks going to ground
from one moment to the next in the old days the cry of a child
might have torn me from the mine and off I went into the next
room, thirty years ago, I extricated myself, I was extracted from
the vital wallowing, but in what kind of a state, my soul scraped
inflamed, mind left behind, stuck in the mouth of the den

and thirty years ago, I sped, mindless, forced—to the side of
the child, the only obligation to which I deferred, giving in to
the fear of a punishment whose self-flagellation would in the
end cost me more than the loss of energy caused by the lacerat-
ing displacement of my body from one room to the next. Thus,
in the old days, I deported myself, to spare myself. Now only a
maternal deathbed could disrupt my frenzied sacrament. "No
one can see me" and no one has ever seen me in a trance and it

is better thus. "No one can see me" I told myself to shore up my total absence of shame, fortunately no one can see me, fortunately the thought-of-my-mother has gone to the market along with my mother, that's why no obstacle to the necessary sabbath, more powerful than any convention.

You would recognize us (frenzied writers and myself) in the body of the cat whose spine paws tail are so tightly coiled by the mental covetousness awakened in them by the thought of prey that every fraction of a centimeter hums with an electrical charge whose effect is to contain all bounds under the skin, here life and its suspense touch.

This tension which takes the mind with body in tow to the brink of death, we know, how we know I don't know, it eludes the social contract, it crosses the invisible but wall-like line, thick perceptible to your hands to your forehead to your footsteps, which separates what is universal acceptable human from the unacceptable. Perhaps, I told myself, on a day a little less mentally searing, a week ago, when I was wondering at these seethings, it's that there is a kind of death-and-gore effect, involuntary but undeniable, at moments when the Crisis takes over: no place for anyone else around the bewitched, which in fact amounts to a sort of virtual assassination. Annulation reigns. Everything is wiped out, annulation, annular, there's only circle, annulus, ring, secret message.

Hence the crazy multiplication of notebooks: what seems mad is on the contrary the effect of keeping madness at bay, an attempt to loosen the stranglehold. But the means of defense itself is taken hostage by the trance it wants to escape. Only a miracle from the outside will release the creature back to its element. Its efforts to free itself hasten its demise.

What is even more confusing in my search for the sheet of paper that I've convinced myself might be the shibboleth is the page numbering. All the beginnings are numbered 1, 2, 3 (never more) occasionally starred, or perhaps ABC, but since each time I start a new notebook I believe that this is the one that is going to take over, I relapse into naïveté, this one, I think, is the real one, the good one, the first one you don't expect me to write "fourth" or "twentieth" beginning. I believe in the beginning. I believe in the beginning among all the beginnings. I believe that among all the beginnings that finally gave birth to the first of my texts, the one that dragged itself still breathing out of the chaos, after which came other things as sticky and primitive as the original survivor, and after that those I finally agreed to call books started to turn up, I believe, but without any certainty, that there is one that caused, that made a dint in the chaos, an event among all the events, that deeply nicked the soul. Without any certainty.

What I'm thinking of is this dint, this nick. Of this wound among the scratches.

In any case I believe in an Ursache. *It's around here somewhere. It's not a point. It's not a letter. Besides there is no letter-sign-alone, a letter is always surrounded by all the other letters. A letter is not without its swarm of other letters. But in the swarm there is the cause.*

The Cause is—somewhere in a chaos you need a chaos—invisible to the naked eye—that which brings two absolutely contrary forces into contact—like God's finger suddenly landing, among all the millions of possible surfaces or crevices, precisely on the spot chosen by an absolute violence, why this one among the millions; and the finger of God which has no hand is the Devil. God puts his Devil down: there—which is to say: here. The area around is irradiated, the entire zone is a scene pocked with fateful ricochets. What happens: in the entire area around the point of impact (you don't know exactly where or

at what time God's Devil landed), hundreds of millions of
traces are set down as in a kind of library.

The most ordinary details emit flashes or blinks of some kind,
they cease in truth to be details in order to become signs, mes-
sages, proofs. And it is this peculiar life of what is lifeless, this
sort of speaking, but mysterious but perceptible, that fills even
the most modest objects in the part of the world struck by God
and his Devil, which shows this neighborhood or place, city,
airport, to be a scene with a cause. An originary scene. Every-
thing in it is infiltrated, grazed, a particle of complicity. Gener-
ally the scene is clearly localized. It has an address. In the Bible
too. Earth-shattering encounters have an address. In the picture
there are animals, mammals, insects, moths, rocks, inhabitants,
a fountain or a well. Each element glows and signifies. Nothing
is unnecessary nothing is not fateful. Somewhere in the scene,
in the sometimes extensible but always localized perimeter, is
the germ of Cause, cause among Causes which hits the target,
like the one bomb among all the bombs released that hits the
bull's-eye. The address of the chaos of the Cause of the bom-
bardment: there were several explosions of varying intensity.
The first, which occurred beneath the marble Dome of the li-
brary of Yale University, New Haven, Connecticut, was not
taken seriously at the time, only once it had been followed by a
series of brutal ripostes, coming thick and fast.

The riposte had followed closely, the quake had come after me,
taken the plane and caught up with me in the guise of The Letter in the office of the curator of rare manuscripts of the State
University of New York in Buffalo.

Here is The Letter. It is typed on blue onionskin, single-
spaced, knowing from line one that it will need the whole space
the whole place the whole attention the whole time, knowing

just how long it will be, what languor it will express by means of what sorts of emphasis with the help of which modalizers.

Literature of saying it all or literature of not saying it all? It chooses to say all.

The letter is a monologue staged on light-blue paper. It is (has been) rehearsed. Now it comes forth and acts. The *tone* rings with poetic regret, you might be hearing G.'s voice on the telephone slow dense heavy supple enough and choppy enough to suit the discreet modulations of a lament. So much for tone. (The matter of *the voice* and *the tone* keeps coming back to mind. I ought to do a linguistic study of *G.'s voice*. Today I can say that a *capitalissime* part of his messages was related to *his voice* and the way he could manipulate it. I can still hear it. The insane discrepancy between the heavyweight voice and the slightness of the flesh and bones gave his voice authority.)

It testifies with grace to the torment of the artist who has just been condemned. The sentence circles around regret at not finishing his work, astonishment at being preceded by the end, pity for a third person (the man, the being) cut down in the flower of his youth, and at the same time around a deck chair drawn up in front of the window through which sun pours, where he lies naked, bathed in yellow. It is indeed the lung it says. *The lung.* Everything comes together in this word: fate, death, the duel. It suffers from insomnia. Or maybe it's him. Just two words it says. *The lung.* Coquettishly the letter toys with its *Lung*. Talks *lunguage*. The rest: the long sentences are written only for The Letter, for afterward. All the things it would have liked to tell her on behalf of the one who lies stretched out on the deck chair vested only in yellow sun crowd into her field of vision and cloud it. The young man however condemned he may be revels in the light. On the floor beside him, desperate, a beetle on its back. The young man, desperate, beetle on its back. The man on his back resembles a squirrel on its back resembles a turtle on its back: in the position of death. One would like to help him. Yet *one* must be in a position to help however *one* is oneself in need of help. A flick of the big toenail would have done the trick. But the desperate fellow is busy writing The Letter that you are busy reading. You have only yourself to blame therefore if the beetle is going to die on its back.

Besides, the person who writes me, The Letter says, even if he summoned up all his depleted strength, can only cling to the paper with the help of a pencil. Besides he cannot get up: he lies where he was left flat on his back, poor beetle, by the sudden and heartless departure of the person to whom he is going to send The Letter. Whereupon along comes a lizard. Nature has arranged things for the best, so has God and so has Literature. The beetle lies in the path of the lizard. Everything leads us to think (1) the beetle's goose is cooked: it has stopped moving; (2) the lizard is a *lézarde*, a crack in the marble wall of destiny. Did they argue? Reject one another? Attack one another? But the *lézarde*-crack in skittering over the inert beetle with a sudden twitch of the hip smacks *the wee little beastie* as Robert Burns would say, says The Letter, flipping it upright. The beetle stays dead for five more minutes. Just when the man is about to scoop it up on the blue-washed sheet of airmail paper the beetle scuttles off to the right of The Letter and exits the scene alive says The Letter.

However that's not at all what I wanted to tell you says the Buffalo Letter, but this:

I was reading this letter like plunging into the depths of an enchanted forest at every step wanting to turn back the retractile forest contracts its horribly leafy mass on you go thinking of all those rats and all those squirrels caught in the trap of an experimental *double bind* and afterwards uselessly of analyzing the dangers: go left and there's the void go right and you drown death on the left death on the right, whereupon anguish wells up in the little body wells up on the left—wells up on the right— pregnant with images of abyss and tide, and thinking of all those creatures who can only escape death by suicide suddenly the squirrel's heart breaks. I was reading the letter as if gripped by two kinds of paralysis, on you go telling yourself it is all a dream you want to believe this but it isn't a dream the dream is not in the brain, you are yourself in a narrator's poisoned dream, if you looked up at the sky you could make out the mesh of a membrane, a net, but you don't look up, it's all you can do to creep along the rails of the single-spaced lines belly on the ground.

It wasn't a letter, it was a tunnel. All along the trench portholes gave onto crude and distant scenes, the only flickers of light along the way are obscene "I am naked on my chaise longue," "a naked man slumped on a deck chair." I could feel a slight swaying I was on a boat without railings big as America and built of suffocating bottlenecks and narrow straits stretched out into damp corridors narrowing toward fake doors, the whole country vibrated and pounded at the temples of the immigrant I felt myself despite myself to be.

I wanted to throw it out but just as I was wanting to, desperate with the lack of air and nauseated by the little flock of phantasms twitching their paws, I read these words:

". . . you're going to want to throw away this letter away, don't do it, I beg you. Consider the state in which I come to you, think of the twenty-five years of traveling I have just accomplished (make it fifty since I am Jewish) when I meet you at a lucky bend in my road and just at that moment it is too late, everything comes to me and escapes me the same day, my dreams are loaded into an ambulance, I cannot cry out at least let me bid you farewell, nothing cries out in me any longer, I am done like a squirrel that misses its leap for the first and therefore last time in its life and I only learn that I am upside-down on my back when I see your feet right up close to my eyes. I am not yet dead since I stroke them, or so I imagine—

"The essential things escape us. At this moment you weep, I know it by virtue of the divining power of fear which serves me as wit, soul, rudder, ever since the hospital handed me my sentence . . ."

With the feigned composure and indifference of someone who fears seeing fear and distress unmasked by the hypnotist I did not throw away The Letter. A Letter is nothing. Nothing but a facsimile. A Letter is a poisoned weapon. A Theater of obscenities. *Lying on the deck chair in the morning naked half in the sun half in the shade.* Nothing but a Letter.

"What are you going to do now?" The Letter said or perhaps wondered or perhaps inquired of me, equivocally: "And now what are you going to do? *You*—was that a *tu*? Or was it a *vous*? Intimate? Or polite?"

It's the end of the holidays as life: all of a sudden it's back-to-school in the Drama Department. A Decision is going to have to be taken, I was thinking, soul hunkering down under a leaden sky. I am about to be knocked for a loop by a Decision. Who up there wants to drop a Decision on me? Aerial attack. A sense of Neveragain. I didn't know that I didn't know. Right up to the Beinecke, mental drifting, never before experienced. It's a shiver of imminence. Of the word *imminence*. Hard on the heels of the word *immigrance*. Dogged by the word *imitation*. A feeling of *imitation* of destiny.

The subject feels increasingly segmented. You don't understand yourself. You are a place. You get lost in it. In the Library, I recognized the books but not myself. I turned up in my place, I sat down, and I was struck with disjunction. I saw myself make spelling mistakes a few words away from me. It will pass I told myself and I was starting to fear this It.

I had been replaced.

I have been replaced by an imitation of myself, without my being able to decide whether I am the semblance or the reality. I was drinking coffee. Never have I drunk so much coffee but I was convinced it was me drinking the coffee.

I am friendless. I am childless. It-has-been-months since I looked out the window. The books: my windows. Perched on the lap of Professor Oscar Silverman of Buffalo, knees as welcoming as the dumb patient knees of my London uncle Jackl Feuchtwanger upon which ten years ago I took refuge from Algeria, I reread The Letter and I sniffle. Not since kindergarten had I cried sniffling. In still-bombed London, affected by the scent of war and ration tickets, I blew my soul into Jackl's ample welcoming handkerchief.

I read The Letter. I cry and sniffle. I let the books drop.

I'm deserting. Or the opposite? I enlist with the ghosts.

In The Tale at that point there would be a close-up of the stack of books I was going to read that week that I let drop. The camera *travels* over one of the volumes lying on its back like an upside-down beetle, squiggle of legs, desperate. It is *Letters to Milena,* which I have never read. One would be able to read the next line: *Consider the state in which I come to you, think of the thirty-eight years* but the picture moves faster than the gaze. Who is Milena? I was about to ask Professor O. S. whose bald pate is a constellation of freckles, just then The Letter came along. Who is—?

(But I lose interest. Pity.)

In the next scene you see me arriving at the door of the King's Crown Hotel, place: New York. I enter. I am friendless. I am childless. I have no books—"only two weeks," I send on a post-card to Silverman back in Buffalo. "In two weeks he goes into the hospital. A tumor." I toss the card into the postal pillar-box. You see me cast an anxious glance around, right to the sky. One is always afraid of being caught in a tactless moment by some secret witness. I am ashamed to have *written* what I think: "Only two weeks."

I am already in *The Hospital*, a devious, difficult chapter, but I don't know this yet.

That afternoon perched on Professor Silverman's lap I weep all the tears I'd never been able to weep: for the death of my father, for the death of my son, all the tears dammed up for fifteen or so years pour from my eyes and blind them: I believe I am afraid of the idea that a stranger could die without being bathed by foreign tears.

Each morning led off to the Library by my mother's strict mind I continue to work.

On the eve of the fifth day without any declaration of war I jump out of the maternal path and betake myself to the King's Crown Hotel.

In the old days I liked *destiny* a lot, the word. Try as we may to believe to make-believe to want to believe we believe things overtake us. Now I know that *destiny* is what we call a random combination of omnipotence-others. The word is reassuring: the chain of events is terrifying.

On the one hand the combination of magic calls coming from scenes and times so distant from one another that they re-mained apparently separate even as they made their secret way by psychic pipes and channels along the nucleotidic vessels unsuspected by me toward the chance meeting point where the accident in my emotions would take place, among which I herein note: (1) the letter *G*; the association between the names—tenderly loved element of the Georges and of Gregor's unrecognized name; the impossibility in 1964 still for me to say the words beginning with the sound of *G*: *j'ai* and all the other angel-words in *j'ai, gé, jet, gel,* and so on, instinctively I always tried to avoid any upsetting contact with the letter G but it is everywhere in disguise in the French language; (2) illness at an early age and sudden death preferably pulmonary or by choking, asphyxia, suffocation,

would not have sufficed to produce the event of my about-face. Terrible event of a great perfection, leaving no room for any other occurrence.

It needed *on the other hand the combination of this combination* of internal elements—themselves preceded by ancestral elements conserved in the silence of my DNA molecules about which I hadn't yet been informed—with an external element of unique and totally accidental power for the sender had no idea, not knowing me, of the effect The Letter would have on me. *The Letter* come in truth from the unknown-to-me outer limits of Literature, freighted with all its secular and subterranean powers. Letter from a Jew-calling-himself-Jewish loaded with the millenary powers of a world with which I kept up a relationship of banishment. Letter that was the very incandescence of Literature, its scandal, its quintessence, its racking cough, The Lava, that moment when the torrent still hesitates as to whether it will become the root of a work or merely a night of tossing and turning.

I AM NAKED

So I took the plane for New York, without arguing with myself.
Maybe it was the train. A letter that offends one side of me.
The side closest to my heart, which takes after my mother and
father for its prudishness or modesty. At home we may go
around naked. But nobody *says*: "This morning I am naked on
my deck chair." Crude, the letter, on the one hand, cruel on the
other—which to my horror landed on me, and what's more, I'd
been read.

Scrunched into the narrow seat of the American machine I think
of the giant bombers roaring over Asia. Everything good or bad
that America looses on humanity. Still today. Always still.
Bombing. Scrunched up Bombarded.

I didn't know him. Along comes The Letter. I took it for him.
Because of The Letter I never knew him. Never again did I have
the possibility of accessing "him." I kept it at arm's length. It

too repelled me. Still today I feel the effects of defoliants falling out of the blue. I was in front of The Letter—The Letter was his author. I didn't want this love (I didn't want love either). But The Letter enveloped it blew hit shattered everything in its path. I responded to the letter.

In each of his letters he speaks of his Letter and similarly The Letter speaks of him, it's a race, at every moment The Letter is in danger of catching up with him, of denouncing him, of denuding him and more than once it does. As for him he watches over it, he spies on it, he warns it, he denies it, he crosses it out.

You never know if The Letter is from him or the other. The Letter seems to be indissociable from the deck chair. The deck chair is its double. The double of The Letter but also him. It figures. It is in the form of a scaled-down body.

The deck chair is perhaps his x-rayed body. Or sculpted. Or what it would become once the flesh decomposed. A transfigure of his skeleton.

The deck chair is the place, the setting. The deck chair is the perfect prop. It can be changed in a trice into a frame for a photo, a ladder, a bunker, an airplane, a rack for torture or a painter's easel, a fan, a dried eagle, into a reading lamp, a servant, a movie screen and many forms later, into a woman of very different kind at long last.

He toys with The Letter as with the door, says The Letter: for you mustn't forget the envelope, the work and the acting, the scene, envelope and Letter act out for each other: he is always taking The Letter out of its envelope as if he had received The Letter and not written it as if he had sent it to himself, he reads it, he pretends to add three words, he puts it back in the envelope, the envelope doesn't believe this and rightly so: he puts

The Letter in its envelope into the pocket of his pants. As if the pants were The Letter's envelope or as if The Letter's final destination were the pants. It arrives in the pants goes off again and comes back almost immediately several days in a row.

One Thursday during these goings on—each day of the letter he writes more and more to his pants it would seem—it seems that, in order to be done with it, all of a sudden he strips off his pants. Then he writes the famous sentence: I am naked on my deck chair.

At this point The Letter is destined for the other since there are no more pants to take the place of either the mailbox or the receiver.

The deck chair is necessarily (with) him.

Even today I circle around this sentence. Time has not in the least reduced its unpleasant force. The minute I received it I rejected it. But just as we could not leave room 91, as if we were ourselves its number and its mental state, so I have never been able to rid myself of that letter in which the sentence I am naked *had been engraved by some mystery whose intensity has never stopped growing—*

I have gone so far as to convince myself that everything that has happened to me, charms, witchcraft, guilty conscience, fear, Everything started when I got that sentence in the eye. I should have got rid of it right away like a foreign body. But I didn't—

Only an angel without sex can in all innocence write such a naked sentence. This is what I told myself but I thought something else. Only a devil can write a sentence that, if it were not absolutely innocent, would be utterly indecent. I pleaded for the angel and against my revulsion. If a woman writes "I am naked on my deck chair," such nudity promptly conjures up all the clichés of feminine nudity, the receiver must read an opening into it.

If a man writes "I am naked on my deck chair," you no
longer know what to think. 1. The statement introduces the
diary into the correspondence. 2. The statement transgresses the
boundaries of a certain genre. It is a modern statement. 3. Does
a naked statement call for representation? Personally I pictured
nothing whatsoever. The word naked brought on myopia. From
the word naked I entered a state of myopia right to the end.

As an angel innocent of linguistic and cultural traps G be-
haves as if he had no sex. All the same sex is there. He writes
this to a woman. Perhaps he is acting as if he were a woman.
Writing to a woman. But since he is not a woman the sentence
represents something else again. What can we say about the deck
chair? Does the deck chair have not have a sex, a gender an
orientation, a use, attributes? Everything perhaps hinges on the
undecidable definition of the deck chair, a discreet and all the
more insidious figure of the hermaphrodite; in the transgression
of the literary genre; in the transgression of the sexual genre.

I should have known the devil by the deck chair.

Letters were your weak point says my mother, as for me, the
genius who sent me special letters in which he spoke from London, bird's-eye view, of rosebuds, mine, in 1933 while I was in
Berlin, in a trice I broke off all contact with him. You don't take
after me says my mother, it's not my fault it's the fault of the
ancestral letters of your paternal DNA. The letter from yourfather dictated by him a year after his death in the hand of Alice
the psychic right away I saw it was from somebody else. I always *e-li-mi-na-ted* shady characters says my mother: I send
them packing. *"E-li-mi-na-te* is the elixir of common sense."

(Here or higher up insert the scene in Grand Central Station. It
remains set apart and ringed with fire, to emphasize its extraordinary imaginary or rather imaginal importance. Superb scene

to film but it will require thousands and thousands of extras. The leitmotif borrowed from Coleridge *In Xanadu did Kubla Khan/A stately pleasure dome decree.* That's it exactly: an immense cupola of solemn glass. Above the platform farthest from the center a huge carved eagle. It doesn't fly off. The building is so colossal that the thousands of travelers slip on the marble like lines of rodents. Time is also gigantic. The lines in front of the counters become nonhuman. I follow the anonymous. No station in Europe will ever have these Valhallic dimensions. Vultures doves Coca-Cola. All the proper nouns stolen by many-citied America now from *The Odyssey* now from the Indians. I myself am passing from Buffalo to the Circean isthmus.

Suddenly from the depths of the hubbub the thud of a body toppling onto its back. You see: a woman's body struggles with the demons. Like the twitching body of one of the possessed pigs after Jesus intervenes in Grand Central Station, Gerasene.

The superposed bodies twitch frantically: the demons have been transferred. Scapepig. Scapewoman. Chains and fetters understood but invisible. I remember. Upright stiff with fear you can tell from the dilation of my pupils what I think of this vision: a primal reminiscence of the anguish of a desperate beetle tied up on its back or maybe a premonition of Act II scene 3 which is rehearsing its chain of events and maledictions on the marble of Grand Central Station. The line half-circles around the possessed. The line swarms around the body like ants and the herd pours down the majestic staircases toward the ticket counters. At every instant a train flings itself whistling through the marble rooms, the woman makes her complaint in contortions, trains pass in the shape of gigantic lizards, climb in gigantic bolts of lightning to the glass sky and take off called Phoenicia Albany Gloucester Syracuse Chattanooga Lear Duncan Appomatox Peoria Wichita Topeka Oklahoma Odessa City last City Hades City USA. The Erinyes are coming! They are coming to see the year die of fear. Erinyes City, Persephone, you can hear them buzz as they touch down legs sticking out of the undercarriage onto the celestial vaults distinctly: *End of the line everyone is going to die everyone down underground.*

Did you see the escalators? They rise at forty-five-degree angles. Everyone is under glass. The world too, in the bell jar. Everyone says "Grand Central" these days. Another shortcut. Neither Station nor Terminal: Grand Central,

everyone recognizes the copy of the Hadean structure. Grand Central Infernal. A huge waiting room under glass. The sky too is under glass.)

—It's because he was going to die I say

—I'd send him packing says my mother

—It was one of Kafka's letters I say

—At the first special letter I always e-lim-in-a-ted, says my mother.

It is difficult to say you started to be in love with someone overnight the day you heard this person threatening to die and to be dead soon, it's impossible to think this.

You do not start to be in love. You rush into love. You throw yourself headlong. You have no desire to be in love. You are at peace. In prose. Sheltered. No plans to be in love with anyone. You're not running a temperature. Not on the edge of a cliff. No future in sight. Nor fear. Then the Thought of death utters a great cry of surprise, in a trice everything turns head over heels, high in the sky falcons announce the news, time has adopted a new look.

You think nothing. You have been flung to the other side yelp the forewarned animals. A crazy punishment, eye for tooth tooth for eye, you might think. All of a sudden love poisons you. Choices flee. In fear and dread you are in love with the person you didn't like. You'd not have liked to love him you love him more than yourself, over and above love you love someone you don't even like.

A kind of suicide you might say. The suicide wind pushes open the window the suicide wind rips the lashes off the shutters you throw yourself into the wind to run away from the idea that you could kill yourself you dive headfirst as a gull with broken wings twists and turns toward the cessation of its pain.

Animal metaphors surround us. You think nothing. You jump, you leap. You don't love you fall. Along come vultures, wounded doves. Soon the squirrels will halfdie in Central Park.

Without death as promised, one would not have loved. One might think: you will (only) love this person provided they die. The love wouldn't go on for too long. Love may be all the greater for its brevity. one counts on the person or on death to keep its promise. But not one of these thoughts would ever have been thinkable or acceptable insofar as they lead to crime and to destruction. Then do you have to think loving death and dying? You can't think this. Or is it suffering loving loving as suffering you cannot want to. So you have to think loving suffering without wanting to. The word *vouloir to want,* let it echo: *vouloir: Vous loi loi loi loir*: You law law law loir. Similarly the word *sanslevouloir*: withoutwantingto. You might go as far as wanting to withoutwantingto.

That's it exactly: I withoutwanted: *je sansvoulais*. But not yet the force to discover the existence of the word. Instead of which, I lost consciousness of my usual spaces I no longer recognized my slopes, my hills, I entered a harbor with the feeling of having taken the wrong door without the least hesitation.

One may think: one flings oneself into love to oppose death, to chase it away, one has to, one owes the dead that which one does not owe the living: life.

Or is it perhaps that one owes life a life. Having failed to save a father or a child from death maybe one has to save the next person who calls for help in the place of the child one didn't know how to save. One won't let oneself venture into all these zones of thinking. They are so entangled crossed cut contaminated that one can only botch up the meaning. With their incessant brouhaha they press at the walls of the heart.

In brief, an *engulfing.*

In 1964 unawares

I was in love with a one-eyed docked wolf.

America: anything can happen. Anyone can become a hero or somebody or dead. I didn't see the image of Gregor bring about the total reversal of my plans in my thoughts I saw the sepia photo of a young poet banished to Siberia, Siberia City, had I wanted to isolate the idea linked to my bouts of weeping it would have been: (1) doubt as to the purity of my soul, which had no desire to be heroic; (2) shame at not having experienced such sorrow and tears two years earlier at the announcement of the death of my son, hence the shameful idea of a belated tearfulness over the death of my son, who in leaving had set me free to go back to my lovers my books my manuscripts.

But not having time to think this out, not having read Freud, never having studied my image in my heart I leapt on the first train or plane, I rushed to the letter, to death, literally. In I went.

I can no longer remember anything about the face of the person who pulls me out of the library. I obeyed the voice in the letter.

It was not *his* letter nor *his* voice, it wasn't him it wasn't me, of this I was unaware.

THE CHARM OF THE MALADY

—Was there *something special* about him? my brother auscultates me.

I wanted to explain to my medical brother what had taken place in the way of mental illness on the ward of my psyche. (Setting for this consultation: the world beach sporting the colors of grandiose old age brightened by the genius of youth the beach white gray cloudy immortal as aging gods, this is the spot I chose to anchor April to the mast my brother.)

—Good-looking? calls my brother between the flaps of wind.

—Literary, I cry in the direction of my brother's mossy ear

I try "good-looking" on for size.

—I didn't *find* him handsome, I was thinking, nary a flash of lightning from his face, nothing like a bolt from the blue no sublime or mythological visage superimposed itself on his, his was a visage without figure, body not big brow high skin white as a woman nothing special other than a discreet non-beauty but I didn't find him ugly I was thinking, this would have been to find him otherwise beautiful, to tell the truth I didn't find him, no seeking no finding,

but met up with in appearance, in pallor. In the shape of a name and the sound of a voice behind which he remained ghostly and a little rusty.

He was missing a tooth, I say. I recall. He dared. To have a lost tooth. I recall I admired after a moment's hesitation the calm of this hole. His hair? Too fine. Like baby hair persisting, an error of nature, a genetic deprogramming like too much hair, residual, doomed, totally out-of-date.

—Strapping manly a baritone cracker of jokes? chuckles my big baritone joker of a brother.

—Ill, I say. The illness substituting for charm I must confess. Not to forget I shouted between the wind the malady, love as malady and vice versa the malady as cause of the malady of loving. The malady I say as a substitute for beauty. Makeup artist with interesting masks. Sick, I say, I believed.

White bread sick before baking, unborn bread, floppy, shapeless, limp, raw dough prebread state prenatal. In the beginning of the first part. But in the second part, paradoxically, back from his sojourn with the dead the pork-butchered unstitched stapled sliced up reduced hoarse one-eyed, he was tougher, cleaner, like human bread after it's been baked.

—Removed, I tell my medical brother, from any kind of din sparkle or intriguing skill. No beauty spots.—Some kind of mark maybe? A wish?—No auspicious mark on the face or body. Nothing that might have held me. No resemblance.—Luscious curls waves? says my brother. A wide mouth?—None of our childhood banners of beauty I say. Neither by his difference nor in contrast did the imponderable and colorless Gregor evoke for me, or so at least I believe, any of the dazzling heroes with their big shoe-black curls their lips brushed over laughs hinting at the possibility of bite-marks.

Besides he was missing a tooth.

No connection in my opinion with one or another of those adorable effigies offshoots of dead oriental religions making a comeback from our childhood days at the outdoor movies in the shape of a very masculine feminine man or vice versa in the shape of a very feminine virile woman, conjugated creatures doubly disturbing who are the unrecognized survivors of the fertility cults celebrated on the beaches of Oran during the war. In our blind nostalgia we loved them we would pronounce as believers their blind actors' names which embodied unknown to all the fatality of a happiness abolished except for a couple of hours of cinematographic dreamland. No church bloomed up around Gregoros no temple that was a loaf of bread left to bake in the sun on his columns. Except perhaps, but out of sight of my weak eyes, the door, on the back right, at the corner of a stinking pot-holed lane, a building set back, disguised in rubble with an oil lamp called synagogue inside. This was out of sight. I passed the building and didn't see it, I was watching where I put my feet the street was littered with detritus and shit. I did not lift my heart toward the radiant chest. You never do see the presence of a gleam of memory in the unknown person you accidentally love. And yet perhaps we flung ourselves at his façade faces pressed to the window of this visage the way an insect fluttering toward the light receives the command to fling itself into the flames. And yet a few ordinary words in a Yiddish that I didn't speak but could recognize had lit the little signal light fatal to fireflies. *Stehte Boche. Consider the state in which I come to you, the 28-year journey I have traveled (and because I'm Jewish, another, much longer one as well) when, at what appears to be an accidental bend in the road, I see you, whom I never expected to see, especially now, so late,* it is so late, he said, when I meet you at an seemingly accidental bend in the road you whom I never really expected to see, especially now, especially so late.

—You loved a Jew—you? my brother asks us—

But how shall we respond to a question whose every word is a thing that is beyond us, did I love a Jew, did I ever love, will I ever love, would I ever have liked to love, would I ever have hated to love, a joo, a woo, a flew *un ju un jui un f un fi un fui* a thing so deep dark lost in the forest that never for a single second do I see it I hear only a rustling.

Sometimes I feel we live in a room at the top of King's Crown Hotel with two facing doors; each of us holds the doorknob of our door; at the bat of one of our eyelashes the other is already behind his door. You will reopen it, since it may be a room that cannot be left. If the first was not like the other, he would remain calm, preferring not to pay attention to what the second does, he would go about ordering room 91 Nine One as if it were a room like all the others; but instead you work your door like the other; occasionally even both are behind their doors and the little room remains empty), all that in English, *j'eprouve parfois l'impression que nous habitons une même chambre en haut de l'Hôtel King's Crown avec deux portes qui se font face; chacun tient la poignée de la sienne; à peine un cil bouge-t-il chez l'un l'autre est déjà derrière sa porte. Il rouvrira car c'est une chambre qu'on ne peut peut-être pas abandonner. Si le premier n'était pas comme l'autre, il garderait son calme, il aimerait mieux ne pas regarder ce que fait le second, il ferait régner l'ordre dans la chambre 91 Nine One comme si c'était une chambre pareille à toutes les autres; au lieu de quoi il travaille comme l'autre de sa porte, il arrive même que chacun reste derrière la sienne et que la petite pièce reste vide.* All that repeated in French as if it went from one room to the next.

So no one was there to see the Torah, which keeps its distance from the emotions, slowly emerge from the shadows and glide and roll to the center of the stage where it pivots, emitting superhuman gleams. Even the camera is put off by it. You understand that in room 9, 1, without anyone's knowledge *the soul of the Tale* is lodged. Was there any *like?* In 1965 I hadn't the least idea.

Do you recognize it? I ask my brother:—Who knows? The angel of death enters the hospital room where the Jews and the dying are stretched out together all mixed up, the dying Jews the dying non-Jews the Jews dying the non-Jews dying the angel of Death gets mixed up in it naturally: is there a Jew in the house? Says he. But at this time of day everyone is reflecting and in all frankness who could answer frankly? In this case nobody responds.

To be perfectly frank as far as I know I've never loved a Jew I say but I could be wrong. My brother either. My brother as well.

The ravenous passion that rips at my guts the bloody lip-smacking sweet Racinian passion in which all the characters are actors whose sex is double, this I experienced during the duple time of war when I and my brother as well favored a reincarnation of Shiva called Victor Anna Mature Magnani an actor actress or an actress priest of the divinity of omnipotence-others, when I saw the one I saw the other when I loved the first I loved the second, it was love on the spot, to the second, still today we love them on the spot, as if feeling life slip away, at the very beginning, infancy of death, we hastened to love them together once again because of having been so utterly loveable mixed up when, instinctively forming the secret society of the passionate innocents, we ate the same bread and drank the same milk.

Whereas the figure of the young man still sitting sipping his coffee in the Beinecke has no curls and no color. Come from New York and not from an extinct religion. Conventional. A classic

—Handsome? says my brother

—Lackluster, I say.—Shoulders?—A little hunched I say. On the other hand the world spontaneously combusts, speech lights up in the lifeless, in our wake full moons rush to rise in the windows of yesterday's shabby buildings, it shines baby teeth baby legs thin faces raked with disappointments avenues tiled in gold and shit all of it glitters and plays the saxophone. Loud blood beats time for the fluttering wings of the inner doves. The center of the world is here where our hands cross on the corner of 5th Avenue and 42nd Street on the steps of the Public Library.

Yesterday I was scared he'd waste my time. Now I shudder at the thought of how little remains. But two weeks in silver and gold are worth their weight in Apocalypses.

A medium-sized conquerer. The pioneer with New York luck, a man whose body was a little soft flesh unrisen the real American as impotent power grown brutal and pitiless again let loose in the jungling of Manhattan, trees of steel of glass monstrous groves haunted with greasy papers and chickens roasted weeks ago a zoo full of animals locked in anthropomorphic trances, narrow chest but eyes drowned in lightning bolts brow beaming with the invincible pride that lodges in the skull of the Innocents, the American omnipotence-other Gregor the shrimp more powerful than all the Old Continent heroes put together, the puny self-anointed absolutely invincible go-getter born of a renowned heritage of fame and stars. This time next year the whole world will have heard of him. With his frail hand he rights whatever threatens to collapse. The flying invalid. Adolescent acrobat on the stolen trapeze. Everything you see is his: the stately and crumbling homes of Washington Square; James's portraits are his ancestors; Dizzy Gillespie John Coltrane Thelonious Monk play before you for him though

discreetly, if they merely acknowledge his presence with an invisible wink it's because you mustn't harass the prince in disguise. He himself claps without a sound, all the music is his,
half the works of art are his creation, modesty is the virtue of
kings. The greatest artists you think are hunched. A sign of
mental superiority. Such greatness doesn't like to call attention
to itself naturally. The bridges too. Brooklyn Bridge his as well.
George Washington Bridge. All the bridges his brides, bridges
in songs, monuments of bridges. The next generation will take
the famous Gregor Bridge, but we won't be around to inaugu-
rate it.

On the topic of regret for what might have been, therefore everything, and was not to be, I shall say that against this back-
drop of oblivion the smallest moments immediately and in the
present acquire the heart-rending loveliness of memory. Everything is being replayed in memory already. Each moment, as it
steps up, sees itself gone already. The sky is an unsilvered mirror. You feel yourself seen in retrospect. Regret looks at us and
takes pity. Moments that wouldn't have had the slightest interest under the seal of death change into treasures. A bag of pea-
nuts, ephemeral. The ripped stuffing of the leather seat in the
Italian coffee shop on MacDougal Street. *"The Guggenheim
opens in its Frank Lloyd Wright home."* Five years old and the
brochure is an ancient ruin. Time goes by seven times faster in
America. The archaic is yesterday. Nothing more up-to-date.
All that happened in *NYC 7th decade,* they'll say. But what will
the readers of the next century and therefore the next millenium
call this age you could count on the fingers of one hand? As if
the world and he, its poet and prophet, had exactly the same
definition and exceedingly brief but sublime extent. In Europe I
would have been thinking constantly about Gregor's death. In

America the allegorizing power in charge of all time and all place through simple atmospheric pressure, at the very thought of such a thought substituted, with a cardsharp's sleight of hand, the thought of immortalization, projecting the still living young genius live among the figures in the museum of *famous people who created Greenwich Village.*

Now the reply to The Letter (example of a construction that produces an echo effect and thus an effect of obsession both in the time of the events and in The Tale and of which Gregor's subtility is the conscious or unconscious author).

Bench for bench. The Beinecke's marble bench. (In between time, old Silverman's lap.) To which Central Park's wooden bench responds. The Central Park Poem will respond to the Buffalo Letter—

(this story is in its outside shots blazing summer for the first part. The second part: all icy, shadowy interiors, snows, blizzards)

all this Gregorian City those victories those weighty newspapers, those underground fiestas, those parks as lively as Circuses with their panoplies of magic tricks, standing behind the scrim of cotton gauze blackened by smoke I gaze at you, incapable of moving, the sword of terror pins me to the curtain, such regret. Something elegiac vibrates in the low, melodious timbre of his voice, a great link to life is loosening, he was going away. Not that death was on its way but life was leaving and the author was thinking with sorrow of The Work he would not complete, of the paralysis foretold of Grand Central Terminal. I would have liked to finish writing The Book. I am depicting the dementia of the American Imitation which I have been noting for decades. The dementia is the magic. For in New York Don Quixote is not a poor crank: all it takes is his kind of willpower for windmills to become really overnight Towers sixty stories high.

—I don't want to die before I've finished writing *The American Imitation*; as he said this he burst into restrained mischievous prophetic laughter. I haven't read Cervantes either. But already the City had become the Book of the Circus. I hadn't yet read Ignatius of Loyola nor Isaac Babel nor Bruno Schulz nor Oscar Wilde nor John Donne.

Licence my roving hands, and let them go before, behind, between, above,

below

Oh my America what sad luck to discover you now so late what sad luck, to love you without being able to hope things will grow to their right and proper term it's like going to sea only to be sick of it, he tells me sitting on the wooden bench in Central Park a little ways from Park Avenue South which we have only barely managed to reach, overcome as we were by a sudden fit of coughing ill wind in our sails. And yet we walk as sky walks on earth but bludgeoned by the gusts of wind we double over and stagger to the first bench.

We are dying, *my dear.*

We die each time we separate

Without smiling.

The last time I died was at New Haven airport New York I saw your orange dress depart without turning back, and now I am nonetheless alive. Several times each day we die and we kill each time we eat up our frankfurters without offering their share to the squirrels, we are kings on earth and we betray one another, manna turns into hamburger meat every time we meet one another without smiling. When we have found the author of our dreams we treat him like our game-bird, we round up a few hunters, we surround him we take him captive we vivisect him we turn him into sausages of paper we transubstantiate him into chapter sections for eight years we export him and most of the time by then we no longer know why he attracted us in the first place.

The summer is blazing hot the dress orange, *Here take my picture* and look at it closely, it looks like me, August 15, 1964, and later on you will say it looks even more like him dead, here take my picture my immortal shade, since death has snapped it once and for all.

You're crazy I say, *you are a fool,* I say frightened a photo, no no photo never I say, already a dozen times I'd thought of wanting his picture "before the departure" a dozen times simultaneously thought "no no photo never." In spite of myself I could feel the frightened thought that wanted a picture despite my desire to believe in the lover's purity of my desire. That's when a brand new sort of shame overwhelmed me on the bench: I had committed the shadow of an assassination, I had thought of the person seated at my side on a bench as already dead. That's when the terrifying skeleton of a sort of shame rattled me—in the cemetery with Hamlet—I pick up Gregor's skull *alas.*

I am two fools says the flying young man I'm not a fool I am two fools I am a fool for loving, and for saying so the third fool guesses all.

Draw this gauze curtain for me, take away this New York veil of gauze, neither repentance nor innocence, I am not two fools at all, I see all.

No sign on the i.d. photo of one or the other kind of folly I say to my brother. On which side? Is the folly on the side of the fool or on the other?

Licence my roving hands *donne donne donne* give give give says Donne.

Say Donne get God says Donne Die Dido you're done says Donne. *Take my picture* says God and give me licence to be a monstrous man. In Central Park underneath the subtly magnetic words I didn't hear the harsh sacred salty incredibly dense voice of the most bewitching of poets, and all was Donne's fault, my fault, on the bench. To think I was an English *agrégée,* a professor of English. What to give to someone who offers you his eternal snapshot?—Charity begins at home says my mother. It would appear you owe me the phone bill.

All the time I kept coming up against pockets of resistance within me, little shrewish wiles, a tendency to survive and forget. I had lost my father then my son but I went right back to living my life brought the other son into the world overnight bedded down my life's books my second son the daylight son like a book in the middle of the books now nothing else would come between me and mine my books I laughed as I read there was no more night.

And now what to give this person who says to me: *Here take my picture and I will give you everything.*

FOLLY USA

I'm forever using this crazy word. After the end I went to see my friend Jacques Lacan, am I crazy I asked him *suis-je folle* we sat side by side at his desk and he was leafing through the Letters, what do you think I say am I crazy yes, yes, *donne donne* give give me those letters he says, give he takes. Right away I get up off the desk chair. But as I was leaving I thought about the crazy word *fou* its meaning going swish-swish *froufrou* overhead between the tall windows of the street narrow as Wall Street. Now the crazy word perches on the gutter. And what if I'd used other words? He didn't know *Donne* or *done* either and I said the crazy word in French. *Fou* I say *folle* Yes yes he says in French *Oui oui.*

But *fool* doesn't mean *fou* doesn't mean *mad* doesn't mean *fou* in the non-sense of its senselessness.

—If I think I've seen a scar twenty centimeters long which doesn't exist and which therefore I haven't seen

—Whereabouts? Where was it? says my brother

—On the chest I say to see a long scar that doesn't exist. *Suis-je folle?* Am I crazy? Crazy mad or crazy friendly? *One fool's two fools. One fools two fools.* Am I crazy with one kind of folly or with two? One male the other female? A fool to say it and a fool to see it? Madman to say it madwoman to see it?

—In that case says my brother you're schizophrenic.

Right away I get up off the bench. This is the first time I've heard this word beat its wings crazily banging off walls in the Wall Street bottleneck above my head this word churning the sky.

Say this word schizophrenic and there is no more madness, I don't agree, let's chuck out madness, the fool rises limp-limbed in the concrete walls of the street of Walls, who invented this hard word, you say schizophrenia and your throat gets shredded by small cruel Jesus nails the little bird bones tear my ear drums a word like that exiles you from the company of your fellows say this word and the gate bangs shut on the zoo of thoughts, I am not where you are I say distraught.

—I don't know anything says my brother I'm not a psychiatrist you have to be mad to be a psychiatrist, who wants to be a psychiatrist and exist on the coattails of the dementia of the demented who only ever pay with their excrements you have to be a schizophrenic to want to be a psychiatrist you have to desire the demented. On the one hand says my brother you have a schizophrenic, on the other you clearly see the opaque silhouette of jealousy falling over the x-ray, that's the psychiatrist. Schizophrenia is a kind of pulmonary jealousy, over there you have someone devoured by jealousy. Drop schizophrenia keep mad it's all the same to me says my brother the world is a huge Terminal madhouse, the individual is the person who writhes foaming on the marble platform in the midst of thousands of travelers obsessed by climbing on board. Only the universe ahead of us, side by side on the same bench from Clos-Salembier, Algiers, to here on the edge of the infernal gulf, remains freely planetary. The main thing is you're still here beside me, my chick. To the devil with madness.

—To the devil with reason I say loud and clear in the direction of the idea-of-my-mother, summer 1964 is blazing hot the seventh decade is epic, everything is glass castles with towers rising like imperial States never had anyone seen such a dazzling season. Stories that begin so lavishly in summer are doomed in winter to tombs locked in ice. But in every case the characters of part one are in the grips of future amnesia. Nobody remembers the Fall of Troy, nightingales crowd the oleanders up and down Park Avenue, it's incredible.

I had already tossed reason to the winds before landing in the Beinecke Library, inaugurated right on the dot for my visit in spring 1964, I was already raving mad when I arrived in California, the oleanders and the daturas were already in bloom. Besides no European can enter the United States without leaving his sensible shoes on the threshold. Hardly have we landed our shell is dismantled, the safe and familiar things, habits customs dimensions are confiscated at customs, we set foot ashore illiterate at the first contact we are bowled over and internally deported by a whirlwind of omnipotence-others, not only does the European no longer know the Law but in under an hour we've mislaid the intimate map of ourselves. We have to count on the walking reflex to keep us going. My house is too big. At each step a room hatches its horribly disorderly space. In the dusty corners of brand new rooms telephones leap away croaking with anxiety. Evolution is still underway.

For decades after the end of the play I couldn't set foot in the USA without having to flee before it was too late, the minute I arrived my mental boat would list, I never know whether to be or to flee, all the names say their opposite, if I say United States *États-Unis* I say *Etazuni Et ta Zuni?* Extasunie in America everyone knows that to say Union is to say Secession everything lures you and slips away, any person who walks down the sidewalk believes herself sooner or later fated to be seceded right to the furthest reaches of her mind or perhaps if I am about to say USA it's in French that the English letters veer toward derision, everyone knows this country-empire-state exhausts the psychic marrow of those who pass through it, it's a staggering country of whiplash changes that reverses itself and sets heads with their topsy-turvy reasoning to rolling and all the genres inside out upside down while beneath the heavenly bell jar the body tumbling in twists and turns it hurts to imagine hurtles to the feet of travelers who avert their gazes from the heart of this deranging business.

What if the present were the worlds last night we asked one another about to be lost in the pushing and shoving of airport arrivals where ten thousand obstacles come between me and the bags fleeing on a sly conveyor belt and in the end I completely forget the contents of my memory, and in my head, yesterday so richly furnished with projects and dreams, every inch is occupied by a single word: *Suitcase.*

In the Great Station all is already lost and swallowed up beginning with two European angels, usually the eyes of my soul: Innocence and Guilt. Earth spins, oh yes, but it's around me. Clutching a metal railing, I lift my eyes to a billboard and what do I see? In white neon capital letters a sentence marked with a Catholic cross files by *What if* blinks the sentence What if. *What if. What if* what? This very day blinks by in a single pulse then repeats this very day this very day, *the present day and month were the worlds last night?* Did you remember to buy insurance? And to think I thought I'd thought up this sentence! Could there be thought readers in this palace of the apocalypse? Or had the ribbon of sentence imprinted its words on my brain deprived of its center of command?

Right away upon arrival I'd received the American war cry: Mortal, did you remember to buy insurance?

THE STATUE OF LIBERTY

—Hefty, virile? says my brother

—Impotence stood for power in him. Stretched out on his back beside me, half knocked out by the shock of the fall, inert but alert he watched his impotence detached from him, danger's messenger, he defied it then tamed it, the tamer has broken his back. Look and Remember: here is man, an intelligent animal. Remember too what I have told you: when I have vanquished Illness, we shall repopulate the universe.

My rooster is plucked after this first assault here he is laid low, impoverished, the enemy's beak is sharp, but love is stronger than death, *do not mourn for I am not dead, accept today with tomorrow.* Tomorrow you shall have me. Once I have proved myself, even on a boatload of immigrants even in prison, eyes put out, chained to pillars I will have you. My tooth will grow back again *you'll see.*

A man even if he is the last one off the last boat of Russian or German or Italian immigrants, whether he enters the port of New York by choice or by force is already becoming American.

The proof is the attention he pays his penis.

In Europe, not much attention, it's not a word you say, publicly yes but by yourself at home never. Once in the USA man naturally takes an interest in his *American*: the latter has its ups and downs, its speech, its versatility. In brief: it is free. The *American* is the Statue of Liberty's gift to the newcomer.

—Liberty for the Penis? It is my belief that this beautiful freedom exists pretty much the world over if under cover says my mother.

Another I say. On arrival all men are handed a new puberty. Remember Karl Rossmann your great uncle Benjamin's pal. Remember Benjamin Jonas your little great uncle. A couple of scoundrels with two bucks to their name. They step off the boat and the Statue hands them America in its entirety.

—They must have shipped off the hotheads to knock a little sense into them. A little hard all the same. But if at sixteen you take to thieving with the likes of those good-for-nothings my uncle Benjamin or his buddy Karl do you think you can set them straight again? Maybe Liberty does the straightening? A lovely symbol that unfortunately is not always put into practice but it's the thought that counts. Speaking of liberty, she faces a prison.

—The boat passenger has a hard-on. You can tell by his mirth: close-up on Rossmann's and Jonas's faces, a pair of ogres you'd say. They are roaring with laughter. They are excited. Pubescent, at whatever age.

Nobody went to the USA aside from the bad boys booted out by their families, people went to South Africa because there was lots of work down there with the dried vegetables especially. Unless they were beans? Cereals maybe.

—Some think she brandishes a sword that's one way of looking at it.

—I know there's a sort of halo with pricks. In her hand she grips some sort of sword. I've seen her often I've never tried to remember what she looks like. I think it's much bigger than a human figure. The Liberty is a copy of the other Liberty says my mother.

—For the rest of his days the American receives a companion be he young old rich handsome poor ugly henceforth the man has an *alter ego*, his American, his novel's hero, neither servile nor servant. The penis paddles its own canoe in between the starry banks. It is the descendent of the anxious and adventure-dazzled passenger, yesterday chased away by the father who, from the boat packed with heavy hearts, sees the approach of the monstrous giant silhouettes standing in a row on the coast. And their entire story has already been written by Homer in Greece. But Karl doesn't know nor Benjamin either that Athena him/herself has come from Scamander in wingless flight to light their first American steps across a hollow metal base sheathed in copper.

Some people sense right away Liberty is a travesty. The accomplishment of a dream of an outrageousness unparalleled in the history of art and the world. A certain Bartholdi immigrant born in Metz is said to have carried off the coup of the century. It's too outrageous not to escape the vigilance of American researchers. The most hyperbolic and the most hyperbolizing Nation had as psychic godfather a sculptor specializing in allegorical monsters transported piecemeal and reconstituted on the banks of the world's most promised coast.

A European's first days in America can be likened to a birth, my uncle Senator Jakob says on the very first day, Karl Rossmann, the first friend the exile Benjamin Jonas made as a newcomer totally lost in the United States, had said, whereas Karl had seen himself adopted from the second he set foot on American soil. And he, Uncle Jakob, had added so as not to needlessly frighten his newcomer of a nephew Karl about this birth, you begin to feel at home here (in the United States, that is) faster, says Uncle Jakob, than when you enter the world of the humans from the beyond. Uncle wished to calm his fears. But so utterly

American was his uncle already that to calm the European new-comer he said the very thing that would most terrify him.

He who is born, the new American nude, loses his memory of his previous sojourn on the maternal continent completely. You never see an infant recount the days before him. And by the same token, stepping off the boat from Hamburg, the child leaves his trunk on board, each time that a boy comes from Hamburg he leaves his suitcase on the boat. This moreover was how Karl and Benjamin recognized one other as having the same prenatal origin: neither of them had forgotten the inaugural forgetting. The trunk contains the original sin. You mislay it forever in the colossal hull of the *Hamburg*.

The suitcase is missing. Karl searches for *den Koffer* in the dim narrow deserted corridors whose direction shifts constantly while Benjamin roots in the luggage compartments and boiler rooms.

I miss the trunk, I say to my brother. The awful thing is in a way I think I know pretty much where it is but each time I head for it ghostly but inner hands abruptly shove me aside, mental hands take me by the hand, the shoulder, the knee and push me in a strange direction. I can prepare all I like for the attack the maneuver is stronger than I am. The first three words belong to the Tale. All of a sudden the way there shifts direction completely. Some people think New York is made up of streets that circle and spiral. And this may be true inwardly, you never get anywhere unless you follow the map of the Municipal Dream.

I am irritated by the way the two boys search it's so obvious they don't want to find, they know perfectly well they left the trunk on the bridge and they turn themselves inside-out making sure they never find it. Plus they grow more and more exuberant and superficial. Whereas I sicken worn to the marrow by my whole being's tension toward the trunk, the suitcase, the coffer.

The landing is comparable to a birth in the world of innocent humans, that is, without remorse and without memory, prehistoric and therefore prehuman. But what ought to have spared Karl and his friend their fear is precisely what terrified Benjamin and Karl both: the speed of the acclimatization—but not so speedy, a little slow all the same—which renders this American-birth comparable to a death and more precisely to a murder of one's former self, which one can't call suicide since it gives onto a birth, but very like. Suddenly one sees oneself relieved of one's old outfit, one's old self. One no longer remembers *oneself*. Sooner or later one calls oneself differently: one cuts off one's name. Benjamerican calls himself Ben. One calls oneself by the tip of one's name. Bill Jim Tom Ted Ed. The rest gets stuck in the beyond. Short nicknames says my mother are very economical. You save time. Fred who landed from Auschwitz in Des Moines Iowa became Fred American instead of Friederich says my mother.

All these men with their *alter egos* no one told me. It's *him* America speaks to. Some think she brandishes a torch. That's another way of looking at it.

According to Gregor it's a perch for angels. The crown is flaming swords. Every last night on the raised fist you can see the angel of death alight.

Even a cheap hotel in Manhattan puts on a royal crown to greet theatrically the characters whose story has just begun. You see me arriving in the room where Gregor has just arrived along with the little fake crocodile bag, as future character in the Tale.

The Hotel is the sole setting for the two parts of the play: one like a Shakespearean comedy the other a tragedy.

The choice of Hotel (from the sign right down to the fake suitcase) as setting is a stroke of genius. The little crocodile bag is unforgettable.

Your fatigue fatigues me, he says, *poor fool* he says, vicariously suffering my dreams of annihilation my penis is droopy. (He speaks to his penis in tones of weary indulgence.) *Poor Tom.* What would you do without me, Dick, and I without you?

Why am I bathed in delight and bliss now when I am so poor in time and vulnerable

But it's not the moment to lament he says smiling gently from the toilet seat as I lower my embarrassed lids with the shyness of those expelled from paradise

This morning we shall go and fish up the world in a net of memory and I shall give you it to keep *but first I must move my bowels,* there's a time for everything, a time for bowels and a time for the City.

Why am I not free of shame and prudishness the way he is, when oh when did I lose the simplicity of nakedness, have I ever known paradise? In front of the door to the bathroom in which he does his business babbling like a toddler, rejoicing that his morning BM is round and smooth as a bagel, I hunt, half-hidden by the door, for the place I might have mislaid the key to paradise.

—See a man on the toilet? I don't see the point. I think you're a little nutty still says my mother. You are a big optimist. In spite of being very perspicacious you trust fools. Speech blinds you. You get taken in by people who have the gift of gab and who make me run in the opposite direction. A man on a toilet? I would have e-lim-in-a-ted him.

DONNE IS DONE

Had he not been in a Library

"Speech leads you astray
You get taken in
The friend who talks toilet talk
You should cut and run the other way
Your fidelity astonishes me
Even a Kafka
From the toilet I would have eliminated him
Some people are so happy, when they've had their BM at last
Right away they have to phone the whole world
Hurrah I've done it
I feel light
A pound less—for this morning—I can do up my pants
Being faithful to the shithead, thanks but no thanks"
My mother trilled.

*   *   *

He talks to me like a kind of old age like a drought. With the harshness of Jesus Christ of whom I have no direct experience, a severity I'd never heard speak. Did I love him? I think I thought I did, he made me think about *me* whom I didn't know, I'd never looked my image in the face not in my heart nor in the bathroom mirror

—Look at me. Remember me. *Here take my picture.* Here you see a man who's not afraid of figures, nor of reality. In London in 1961 there was me and Otto Klemperer. The Philharmonic Orchestra. Sometimes trumpet sometimes oboe, for The Three-Penny Opera Suite, *wait till you hear me, won't you be surprised.* Hurrah! I went!

—And what was I doing in 1961? Between one son and the next, at the inconceivable crossing of immigrant with emigrant.

There was the war also. In the war the wars switched place and touched me from close up and far away. There was the end of the Algerian War—my war and that of my brother—my youth and my brother's—right away at the end of our war, as War Suite, the beginnings of the War of Algeria against itself, in which my mother, a year earlier, swept up like a gull on a tidal wave, had found herself deposited behind the bars of the Algiers jail and in her wake my brother.

Right after leaving the Algerian prison I banished myself from France to the USA, a citadel without any windows on the enormous African backwash. Here in New York City everything led one to believe that the country of my birth, unleashed, and its former tamer in a lather did not exist. I never even said the name Algeria any more, as I said. In exchange here in the American circus we have Vietnam for savage war to give you back your terror on the paths of Central Park haunted by spooky uniforms, true and false madmen, military copycats, we

have Dallas for blood and gore and newspaper fodder and on
the frontispieces of airports the same slogans call out all alone
on the superhighway across the Arizona desert: *Don't forget
your life insurance.*

*I've forgotten everything. I remember places without names
and names without bodies. I remember the name of the Hotel
and the slope of the street. I have never tried either to remember
or forget. I didn't know myself I remember I do not recognize
myself in this self over whom all the storms of American bombs
burst. I have taken her place. I am indebted to her for having
preceded me obtuse and disarmed, cast up like someone for
whom dry land is even choppier and more dreadful than the
sea's monstrosity.*

*She had none of what I have. The feeling of banishment grew
until she crossed the last human rivers and finds herself now
beyond Mourning Heights at the foot of Mount Circeo one
morning in the great empty reading room from the dateless time
of the millennia before Frank Lloyd Wright, on the other side
of the concrete wall that keeps the Gift's circulation away from
that of the Poison. See her venture before anyone before any
hour to the tables of the Beinecke Library still littered with the
remains and crumbs of the sacrifices offered up during the night
to the appetite of the dead. She herself coming ahead of the
waking of the dead still asleep in their invisible wasp cells. I am
indebted to her for these extreme solitudes that deport her from
dream to dream in the mental orphanages. Illusions but so
fierce and so well acted that they fill every inch of reality.*

THE WITNESS

In the Columbia University Library elevator we are alone with
Angus Fisher. Like Perceval with the Fisher King: How many
questions I do not ask! Do Angus's eyes look at us? We look at

each other in secret in the elevator of who knows how many secrets.

—*How is allegory?*—*As if it were done.*

Who knows what secrets travel from floor to floor? Ah! If only I could have questioned the author. I might have pictured the scene from the spectator's point of view. Between the first and the seventh floor I stood alongside the Witness. I ought to have asked the question I would have had all the keys. But the elevator, fate, the novice's shyness before Angus Fisher the authority on *Allegory the theory of a symbolic mode,* the divinities of the secret didn't want me to say a word to the guardian of the truth. We were with her, had I known that one must not lack curiosity, but she got off on the seventh floor with Angus Fisher and we went on and right to the end, if I had known the story would come to an end that day in the Columbia Library. But luck was with her. The focus of the scene narrowed, right afterward space shrunk around my mind, I could no longer turn my head to the side, the elevator turned into blinders. But the divinities didn't want me ever to forget the name of the sole witness of the Gregor affair that I have ever come across in reality.

(Perhaps I ought to have put the elevator higher up I repeat that I have some very clear but dateless images and others cavernous, I see clearly the face of Angus Fisher, the Allegory expert. Note the constant feeling of having passed unawares into the Allegory myself,

even today whenever I wonder what an allegory is, I can see the little elevator for three characters held in a pact that is a figure for the just missed meeting.)

—No, no, not the word schizophrenic, the other, no, *the other.*
Here, take my picture and imitate me says Jesus
Don't forget that I am Jewish *Jewish Jesus*

128

Give give but what what to give for still not yet enough?
Give-give *donne-done* at midnight I shall come back
I shall arise in the midst of the stricken and the pigs
I shall rip off the straps and the drips
Meet me at the King's Crown Hotel
Room 91 *Nine One*
The first of January of the Gregorian Era
And I shall give you *Everything*
Everything? Consider that I give you everything since I give
you my word that I shall give you everything
And you, *dear love,*
Have you given *everything?*
—I think so.—Have you given Everything too?
How to know? How much of everything and how many ev-
erythings constitute Everything? Each time I say everything it
seems to me that all of it slips away everything escapes every-
thing save Everything, I fear.
Have you really and truly abandoned everything?
Who am I to follow Jesus?

—Give give says Lacan.—Am I crazy? Well yes, naturally.
The French language has been for centuries so abstract, *tout*
goes back to nothing in particular. Whereas in American *Everything* is more concrete, *Everything* counts each thing you
haven't given.
—And your drawers. Did you check all the corners?
Is there something that you haven't given and that may have
escaped Jesus Everything?
A long coughing spell muffles Jesus's stern voice.
At night I slip to my chest of drawers like a thief. Old letters;
a portrait of me engraved by Friedlander I admit I was still
attached to it in spite of myself behind my back.

I also own I do not burn them. I do not throw them in the trash. I don't tear them up, don't break them. At night I go into the woods to leave these remains of another life that I wish neither to keep nor to destroy under the Oaks. I slip back to the room like a thief who's robbed herself.

Room 91, last floor, last night in the world, the room is a dim allegory that makes *an everywhere* of a little room twelve meters square.

You have to imagine the next cell, the scene takes place in the hospital in which Gregor utterly alone faces Death.

Describe in one page the capital-C Combat. *No visitors allowed.* Picture endless, colorless corridors as in my hospital dreams. Everywhere panes of glass that divide combatants from dreamers. How frightened I must have been! Shout. Shake. Without a doubt. Pray. Surely. Once again insist on my disbelief. Hope. Let us hope. Hate? There is hate too, sour smell of nasty feelings in the halls.

—If I die you will hate me, *my love.*—But if you live—Ssht! The Red Light's on.

Not dead but. He can't speak.

—That motor noise the cassette is vomiting up, what's that?—The lung. The iron lung.

You don't recognize the roar? And those big burps from the motor that breathes in his place?

—It's the first time I've heard a lung pant like this. I listen close as if I could translate the roar of the apparatus into his voice.

—And you didn't telephone?

—The hospital? Never. It's the least you can do.

Not telephone. Don't distract the paralyzed fighter from his Fight. Do not show the person in anguish the anguish of the healthy. Do not barge into the line ahead of the mutilated speech of the lung patient.

—I tell you

(1) Flee the Temptation that draws you where I am not.

(2) Flee the Temptation to approach my hospitalized body.

(3) Hold your tongue, and let me call you.

No this is not the life

One might be mistaken

It is death which permits us

To learn what is most important

For our glory

Are we not for it?

I mean: for it, obviously. To face it embrace it

—I thought life—

—*For God's sake hold your tongue and let me teach you love.* Do you see the confusion?

—It dazzles me.

—As usual you were going to take the initiative the direction of "life" once more and contrary to what Jesus advised you were listening only to yourself, I see you.

One eye open, the other shut, from my hospital bed I see everything, as you can see.

—Yes yes, the confusion, I see.

—You let your mother speak for you. *For God's sake hold her tongue.* Let her hold her tongue, good lord, when you open your mouth we hear her German.

I speak only English now struggling with the calculations and disguises of life, I no longer speak except in English, but what does that mean life, if it's my mother and her way of ju-dging along with the conviction that ju-dging involves using your powers of reasoning to avoid catastrophes.

Enough fleeing enough playing. Death tolls for me, this time it is no longer the mute modesty of my son George nor the choked off silence of my pulmonary father George.

In a single bound I have leapt into the prison of the gift. The dungeon has hidden resources: once the door is locked it grows narrower and narrower.

For months I've been in English in this *jealousy*, in this conspiracy for abnegation and denegation for the abdenegation, *fond woman*, you have joined the plot, room 91 this is its castle, *you exile yourself* here *freely*. Next *you exile yourself freely* in the house of waiting where you conspire in French with your imprisonment.

He wasn't called Gregor. He was called Gregor. Speaking of the
person who waswasnot him, he said he called him called himself Gregor. I try to follow the thread of the improper proper
noun, it is very difficult

all the same calling him I thought I called him himself and
each time I called him it was Gregor I called and he who wasn't
him turned up quickly to answer for him, to interpret and be
him.

Thus he lived one life according to the law of the name he had
given himself in place of his given name and therefore ruled by
Gregor as his proper noun

and proprietor of his thoughts or simply the manager, dispossessed and possessed simultaneously banished by him, the
banned whose existence I never suspected, the bizarre jailbird
of this spiritual adventure, the forbidden, interned, and simultaneously occupied, translated, transferred, completely replaced

by one Gregor by name, whom he had made up on the spot at the time of the Beinecke meeting. How the Gregor had jumped on his back, injected himself into his marrow, in a flash taken possession of the place and expropriated the possessed-dispossessed—for all information about this eventful moment, concerning its speed, physical, psychical, amnesic, elective symptomatic consequences you'd have to be able to interrogate the sick or patients—beneficiaries as well as victims of these *summoned* invasions. For what we have is a phenomenon of self-de-capitation or self-decapitalization, self-uncrowning-with-a-thought-to-self-recrowning, comparable to a graft-fusion of Lear with the *fool,* not only dis-leared but into the bargain delearious.

Which of the two *hims* seemed to him to be himself the grafted the graft the grafter? I shall never know. Either he was *only himself in this duel* of himself with against for in above below himself, like with like and perhaps he was always this duel, over which the name of Gregoros the one who never sleeps keeps watch, therefore wide awake and dreaming, his own Siamese brain, Gregor the one who keeps watch over the one who sleeps.

He himself however sleeps, him first of all if it's him, he himself however sleeps—does he sleep?—sleeps with one eye open, but which one, which one of the two eyes, the one that seems to turn toward the light, or the other that behind the black patch seems to flee it?

Which of the two is the messenger of the other? I wonder if he asked himself the question I myself ask without hope of an answer.

I imagine the heart of hearts: an underground gallery floor to ceiling with shelves; in one vault the Ghost Theater's costume shop a storeroom with very high walls crowded with great steel lockers packed with the forgotten and unforgettable costumes of the *tragedies* and *comedies,* ghostly bodies at one time inhabited by souls with fevered destinies; a grotto saturated with hundreds of cobwebs a good broom would make short work of. But for some reason no one dares to sweep out this factory. Beneath a tent of veils as frail as they are tough Gregor weaves first this one then that, according to whether he is thinking in Hebrew or in English from right to left or vice versa the transformation inverts his meaning, now it is this one that stands for the other, in whom he flees himself or seeks refuge. Refugee, refuger which one is he the commander commanded by the other who the commanded commanding commander?

—Watch me fight bleed choke stab and finally kill death. Didn't I tell you? I only lost an eye in the Combat. Here I am half Samson and the rest is all yours. When I can bend my paralyzed legs and turn my head, whose pain at the moment is gnawing at the bars and my bones, toward you, you will see the face that fighting tooth and nail has made me and you will smile askance at me.

I never looked him in the face
Never tried to draw the curtain
Always lowered my eyes
It is not proper to look at the poet
Either on the potty
Or in the iron maw of a
Breathing machine

And what if you did just the opposite
Of whatever you should have done
What if you'd had another heart in your heart
Auto-immune, that one

This is exactly what Jesus said to Satan
Exactly what Satan would suggest to Jesus
The pair of them cackled on the ledge
Of my window as I waited
Furiously for the mailman
No difference between the two birds, the one simply a bit
bigger than the other but perhaps it was the other that was.

—Look at Saint Julian. Don't stop at leprosy to make yourself
laugh to tears you didn't weep before.

Imagine loving him all the more as he becomes half-blind,
toothless, bald, castrated.

I went all the way to leprosy.

I should have been deadly jealous of that Sheila person who
gave him her breast to help him mime a rebirth on the Hospital
pulmonary ward to which he had been taken half dead and
dumb when he came out of the iron lung. But if I was I don't
remember. The whole world wanted the world's Watchman to
live. And as a torrid heat that purifies the passions in a brazier
of air to the sound of chirping crickets prevails around saviors
who can't save themselves, so the usual feelings sizzled like
mosquitoes at a candle's flame.

On the contrary, I must have been grateful to this Sheila person a middle-aged woman as befits the role, his editor, wet-
nurse, or godmother therefore in New York in the city as in the
hospital, a fantastic person surely, but I don't remember. Only
her name remains, so generic it has always resisted effacement
and incredulity. She's the one who played Mary in the produc-
tion of the play that I've never seen.

I should have been deadly jealous, but this would have been
a feeling from a different sort of story, a novel of psychological

labyrinths, let's say, Proust, Svevo, or Musil even, but we were living a story more like the psychology-free tales of the Middle Ages' ordeals where the characters are bound to plod on, clutching a transparent ladder, beaming

through the flames.

Besides I was too busy picking fleas off myself. The nursing-mother scene reached me in a letter typed on Gregor's machine that this Sheila person who breastfed him in the Hospital deliberately made use of to brighten me up by telling me how the patient who did indeed seem to be dying finally opened his eyes, he was back, he was coming back. A new kind of watch-keeping was about to begin.

And you, have you vanquished your shadows?

I won't tell my brother this scene. Or my mother either. I thought, seeing the letter and Sheila coming back to mind, on Gregor paper.

The film, to whose "nursing the dead" sequence I have just alluded, was shot in a harsh style, bright lights, almost Lutheran to which I subscribed enthusiastically, that's what worries me—

You must picture the Room 91 of January 1, 1965, in shades of black, black curtains, dingy wallpaper traces of New-York-black grime in the little black tub where degenerate New York cockroaches squirmed, their long spidery legs the black vestiges of the good old cockroaches of yore, skeletal semblances of once-plump scarabees, black roaches honed to a thinness, blacks of the unconsciousses whose scratched tubs spawn pipes swarming with explicitly aggressive silhouettes. Animal beasts in truth fossils revived by fear climbcrawl our sides in vain, we shall not climb out of this hellish funnel. In one corner for sure stood the wedding roses high red hard victorious, a black red,

I've totally forgotten them, but in one of my old books it says they were there. I still feel a mute rigidity in the corner of 91. Which keeps me from seeing when at last, pursued by the white harpies of the storm, I crash headfirst into the hundred times conjured-up scene, it's *Patch,* the eye-cover. I accuse myself of having dreaded seeing the concrete cruel blindness a square, a triangle or a circle of thick black fabric, too much like the leg-less body of a roach; my terror explains why I saw nothing other as space than a vague, cavernous bit of Hotel into which I stumbled.

I am sure I didn't switch the light on, "don't turn it on," he probably said, "mind my eyes!" and I myself was blinded by the anguish-of-love I felt in his presence. I don't know if I raised my eyes to his face or when. I saw the eye-cover, did I see it? What did I see? The scrap of black fabric, I couldn't not have seen it naked and black I couldn't want to see it, want not to see it, I couldn't want that: not to want—to see this thing that encloses, one must respect, not (how to resist) lift one's eyes to what doesn't see, an eye, one must respect an eye closed for an eye closed patch for patch or maybe just the opposite. How to respect? There mustn't have been any daylight and still by the light of a bulb. *The world's last night* has begun.

Probably I spend a few days there, but no memory. Did we leave the room sometimes? Did we eat? I can't say. It seems to me I never say boo. I had a sort of patch on my tongue.

Probably I saw him seated on the toilet, speaking in a serene and profound manner at odds with my silent exaltation, going about his business with that simple gravity you see also in Mon-taigne, on the one hand the needs of the entrails on the other the needs of the soul are treated with the same care for their accomplishment. While I turned this virtue into shame for my-self. Never did I have the force of saintliness—seated on the toilet—to speak while reflecting at length upon life as upon

138

death and vice versa, like Socrates in his last moments content-
edly scratching at his leg, seated upon the rim of the lavatory
(this was his usual position) after the removal of the irons.
Never. None of our human things are higher or lower than the
rest. There are divisions and degrees, but with the features of
the same man. And yet me, never. I separated myself. I think I
recall that the sentences sliding across the bathroom's smooth
walls were preaching at someone, the monotonous and sad
voice declared: *she* made off with an ancient and honorable
piece of work that belonged to the poems' author. *She* works a
great deal, being a highly *efficient* person, she gives many signs
of her devotion, all listed in her *curriculum vitae,* she under-
takes nothing for spiritual reasons, for she has *no spirituality
whatsoever,* the sermon was saying and the words *no spirituality whatsoever* echoed and re-echoed. The sermon's drone
seemed to close in on me, it seems to me, I think I wanted to
protest, but I don't think I was able to.

"*Reflect* this spring, *reflect* upon everything you took and
stole away, *reflect* upon your predatory soulless personality."

Was this when my childhood and peace of mind came to an
end? In Room 91 of the King's Crown Hotel on January 1,
1965? Or a few months later in France?

I also see a work table heaped with pins, they are mine, I am
trying to collect them in a heap, to gather them together, but I
don't know where to put them, their box has disappeared, pins
by the dozen and a few needles.

All these prickly cruel ridiculous little events took the place
of my amorously passionate enthusiasms and equally adored
literature. Pins roaches words seething and somber, a radical
exchange.

I haven't the slightest recollection of my departure from New
York or my return home. Probably I was terrified not to know
what it was I was.

It is from Room 91 that I make my exit accused and therefore guilty. Up to then I wasn't. I don't remember my arrival. The idea of self-improvement takes over my life. I set to reading all the books which reflect upon things. I wash my hands. I am sitting in a little room. I read. I try to climb the walls. I wash my hands.

—You are washing your hands, what are you effacing?

—What are you hiding from him who hides nothing from you and shows you *Everything?* I show you my weaknesses, I don't hide the hole in my teeth, I show you Patch on my wounded eye, I do not hide the scar that cuts right through my truncated life and chest from the left breast to the diaphragm, I show you the strength that carries a diminished man beyond the limits of the human.

Yet you, haunted by whom? In your sleep? With your poisoned claw you rake the wound, you strike—urged by what?—neither to the right nor the left of the scar on my breast sign of the victory won *for you* over the archangel of death, and then you strike out at my most tender flesh? In the false bottom of whose cave did you calculate this so precisely ambiguous blow? I read and interpret.

You over there dozy nitwit quit washing your hands and answer for your gesture. How do you explain the gesture that springs from the depths of your sleep? How can you do such things in your sleep? What do you hide there behind the face to face words?

For God's sake turn off the tap and speak

I fight to return to you, I force death back

And you come along and tear at the consecrated signature on my breast

What was being plotted inside of you?

Stop brushing your teeth while I question you

You would kill the man who made death back off?

Or is it the man who succumbs you meant to punish?

—In the darkness and gloom in spite of myself I own up and deny.

—What?

—Everything. Anything. The crime needs a culprit so why not me? Everything is nothing evil and good wed and both at once answer for each other in the matter of the scar uproar.

—What guarantee do I have that you won't start this assassination attempt all over again? You were sleeping. You weren't even behaving yourself!

In the gloomy depths of the self exiled of its own free will to cell 91, in spite of myself I deny and I admit. In my own head I have Doubts about myself which worse luck is not mine but another.

Every five minutes I avow and re-avow a crime I would never have committed, committing these and those crimes by ghostly proxy, someone is using my sleep to mount an attack on the temple. Right on the sacred seam! The room is full of invisible swine. A pack of grunts in the elevator. *Scar, scar, scar* throbs the chorus. Let us enter delirium then.

—I admit the existence of a double whom I don't I admit.

—You don't think I lacerated my own breast?

—No no no no.

—I see myself playing host to a bad dream into which I have fallen, I can't wake up since I am not the dreamer of this nightmare.

I wasn't dreaming. There was no waking.

I realize I say that in order to portray Gregor I am portraying Room 91 or the famous little identity photo which seems to be a true photo, in which the person isn't looked at but looks straight out and sideways at the same time, a phenomenon of looking vigilant. Right from the very first King's Crown this became a set of scenes, which I now see were very well written well directed well put together, for every time these events had a literal meaning and a relatively simple sort of sequencing, but right away they would start to echo one another, repeat, display an anagogical meaning, an allegorical meaning, a homiletic meaning, an esoteric meaning, and each time it all added up to another version of the great myths of human destiny, Gregor appearing according to context in the role of a hero doomed to sacrifice as well on occasion to resurrection, sometimes if, for instance, he was reincarnating Gilgamesh, to a Duel with death, whose outcome was not sublimated. According to whether we were in Central Park (episode of the half-buried squirrel which I'd thought died horrendously suffocated, only its tail remaining like that of a Scandinavian giant left standing on earth as a visible challenge. And after a few minutes of anguish, for I saw in it a cruel allusion to what awaited Gregor, the half-dead had suddenly exited perfectly alive from this burial) or in Harlem (episode of the knife-man who had cut off his own hand which he gripped in the other, an unbearable vision, that ripped the cry off my lips before I could utter it. The number of severed hands in Gregor's brief life, like a sign to warn off the man who writes. He was himself amazed to have known so many one-armed, severed people, men women and children).

But I never knew anyone who had known him and I knew him only in the version concocted for me and whose principal setting, Room 91 in the King's Crown Hotel, naturally bore none of the personal traces that nod and speak to the imagination. The clothes, for the occasion, were the generic garb of young academics. His parents were good, and dead. They were rather sketchy, having no doubt been latecomers to the construction of the scenario. They turned up only to enrich the context and fill in background details. I pass. According to Gregor what remained was the tale of a visit to the Jewish cemetery, undertaken without me, to bid them farewell before entering the hospital. He'd put stones on their graves, and what I got was an account of the stones, plus the scene of the shirt button the rabbi at his father's death tore off so brutally, and with scissors, that Gregor's chest was scratched. I realize this story might have engendered the whole Scar story but perhaps he had the Scar in mind already at the time of the cemetery tale, and had begun to construct a set of subscenes disseminated in time, as if dropped in a forest, but already present, to lead to the Revelation of the Ultimate, that is, The Scar: *La Cicatrice*. A theme of exceptional richness of meaning, at every level and in every way, linguistic for one, language effects in the American idiom (*Scar, Star*), literal, metaphoric, and psychoanalytic: trauma, wound trace, visible or invisible scar tissue that replaces really or allegorically the loss of a substance which thus is not lost but compensated for, mnemonic swelling; at the philosophical level trace, graft, graph, mark: at the geological, geographical, geopolitical level: one must allude to the furrow as well as to the border, all the material, symbolic, immaterial traces evoke vestiges and ruins, all the discourses on ruins in Western culture, all the Romanticisms revolving around ruins, sometimes envisaged as elevations, shard heaps or on the contrary as holes, lacuna, monuments to absence, or yet again to persistence, according to the point of view and affect (of the reader) of the interpreter, the relationships between natural ruins (volcano crater, fault line) and the cultural ruin; presence of the past, splendor of the past, hideousness of the past, splendid hideousness of the past, past of the past, benefits of mourning, lack of a tooth in the upper jaw superficial metaphor of mortality, and so on. Innumerable are the scarred domains.

Besides Literature is scarry in its entirety. It glorifies the wound and recounts the injury.

From the epidermic point of view, *Scar* may be compared with the invisible weak point of Siegfried, a non-scar, an opening for which you need the password.

Had he thought of The Scar for part one's finale the minute he began to compose our story in his mind or had he thought up this bright idea en route but needed to trial-run it in case it flopped? Or had The Scar just popped up unexpectedly shortly before my arrival at the Hotel on the first of January at least in the theatrical form it acquired for this scene . . . ? Did he need time, and how much time, to outline it? paint it? glue it? configure it? I don't know how, for I don't recall having *seen,* that is, looked at *The Scar*—

I will never be able to throw light on it

These questions come to me for the first time thirty-five years after the fact—

Important in connection with Painting.

Add here, or above in the *Sudden Returns,* that he portrayed himself simultaneously as "the young man with a Future, as ordinary man everywhere surrounded with signs designating him for some sort of ambiguous election: prophet? or cancer? and also as artist already very much in touch with the themes of his art, and what's more speaking to me of his Art as of an inner star already familiar and indubitable.

Quote here one of the notes on airmail paper I haven't thrown out that I dashed off on the spur of the moment, as the indirect style and the use of ellipses and abbreviations show, for instance this:

"*His Art*: (Son Art). *Fascinated with Distortion* the word framed and highlighted. *All Kinds: lies* I translate. *Toutes les espèces de distorsions: mensonges* . . . distortions due to modifications of light, distance, etc. Distortion in beings, minds, infirmities, misunderstandings, deafness, up to puberty didn't think, lived. Suddenly mind on the march: great fear when he realizes that his memory plays tricks on him. What he lives is not what remembers. Begins to write at the age of 12, 2 machines. Note mutations, incommunicability—Works on language. Exercise: Take a thought: 2 or 3 months the same thing expressed in 4,000 sentences . . ."

I must have admired.

In truth he was an artist of lying and of Distortion in itself something admirable.

He was also counselor at the Atomic Energy Research Commission under Kusch, of whom I hadn't heard. One does math the way one breathes. On the other hand, writing: work. But all this had faded into the background.

Now the big Sun cancer, solar plexus. Now only live.

He was also Jewish, seemingly.

Nothing stranger for me than these worlds caught sight of through cracks in doors and all put aside until later. After the Combat.

I must have admired the multiplicity of his personas all looming up on the spur of the moment, improvised.

A great modesty prevailed.

THE VROOM VROOM PERIOD

NON-ELIMINATION

My mother is filing checking account statements bills receipts invoices in the Mephisto shoebox and saying:

"I thought you'd met a great guy, how was I supposed to know he was good for the loony bin for starters a Jew an American. Then I realized the things he was promising never materialized. That fur coat, never, totally superfluous and into the bargain inexistent. Never turned up, doesn't bother you.

All those phone calls cost me an arm and a leg.

Always calling and reversing the charges doesn't surprise you.

What surprises me is it went on for so long. When I make a phone call one two three I cut. A guy who asks you to call at those rates, and you're the one who's footing the bill, in other words me. Right from the start I should have been a different person and said: "Not one Cent will I pay. Something else I can't get over. From that impossible character. You accept the unacceptable.

I should have told you about *the first strike.*
One strike, I send them packing.
The first strike was Herman.
The day he said: leave me a bit
Of this tin of pâté
I invite you to dinner
This tin of pâté but
Don't take too much
I want to save some of it for tomorrow
I sent him packing. Without a word I get up and go
I didn't say anything that was it. Don't eat too much of it.
And I *never* saw him again.
From my friends I don't put up with
The slightest faux pas. There are limits
With the pâté I ju-dged him.
I should have told you the pâté story when Gregor was
around
How to behave with a lady so
If you'd got it, you wouldn't have got it
I think I myself being somewhat naïve
I didn't react, I ought to have reacted
That tin of pâté. The fur coat
That never turns up, that's when I knew
Something was fishy. To start with I thought it was the real
thing.
Those packages he promised—cross his heart—never came
The bills I got afterward. As for me
Never would I have let preposterous people sidle up to me.
I was exploited by your
Easily hoodwinked side and thereupon
Get hoodwinked myself is odd
You were always hooking up with deadbeats

In whom you believed. I call them deadbeats
There was always a combination of circumstances
That smelled fishy.
He was a scoundrel and you an idiot
You believed in this guy whom you didn't know was sick
In a different way.
That Vroom Vroom lung machine business.
You heard Vroom Vroom and you believed
He'd *said* lung cancer.
He wasn't all that crazy. What he made up, that Machine
Vroom Vroom, that was pure inventive madness.
How did you do it? To be so credulous? There are limits.
Invented madness—is it madness?
It's true there was a theosophist in the family.
But he had an extremely good heart
Yourfather's family, big-hearted believers.
Yourfather got hoodwinked by promising people
Jewish middlemen in whom he put his faith
Whereas me never, except through you
Did such sums in dollars ever happen
Me, the people who looked promising
Even Jews
I e-li-min-at-ed them on-the-spot
I was incorruptible
You're high-minded always ready to get taken in
Hangers-on, get thee hence! says my mother

But you—*one* letter and you're done for. Who made you so
short-sighted? In a jiffy I see what's up. That smidgeon of pâté
that Herman fellow wouldn't give me
     For me that was it. I'm not up to coping with skinflints. I e-li-
min-ate them-without-a-second-thought.

The hero's bill was over a million. What a horrific business!

—The worst I say is not the bill, it's the painting. The Scar Story I say gives me the creeps.

—I've totally forgotten that story but not the solar plexus. Cancer of the solar plexus, no such thing. Yet another word to put you to sleep, and boy were you sleeping! You're in dreamland, and when you wake up, I pay the piper.

You can't tell a genius from a liar. Whereas I, the letters of the dubious genius, I don't even open them."

(I was exhausted. I won't take this any further I thought. I won't write this horrific book I tell myself)

You always keptgoing says my mother. Whereas I avoided all disasters because at the least step over the limit I e-lim-in-ate. I almost married Wertheimer Alfred. I called a halt in the nick of time I'd have ended up in a Kibbutz milking cows. A marriage made of gold, biggest store in Osnabrück. An honest lad, tall and thin, with lots of good points. He was awkward. Awkwardness has its limits as well. He came to me in Paris wearing shorts. Wanting to go to the Opera. Without bringing a pair of pants. Already this was beyond the limit. I forgave him the shorts which was my first error. When I said that with him I wasn't going to be married, he didn't in the least understand.

The cause was a group of causes:

1. When he kissed me he thought he should let The saliva flow. That was revolting.

2. He asks me to sew a button on his fly. Being very modest, I found this too much.

3. The Opera in shorts was the first cause.

In short this Wertheimer was a show-off with nothing to show. A dreadful story that I put a halt to in the nick of time.

Whereas you have never known where to call a halt to the dreadful Gregor story. A guy who writes: "I am naked," first cause, you keep right on. Second cause: the fur coat. Third cause: the Vroom Vroom machine. Fourth cause: the horrific bill. A ghost, says my mother, but the bill really and truly needed to be paid.

I close the account, your cause was full of causes that you didn't want to see and look at.

No way out of the dreadful Wertheimer story. I was ashamed of myself (1) to have e-lim-in-at-ed him but I felt the necessity. I wasn't about to get married for the sake of getting married. I was ashamed (2) because I shouldn't have gotten involved in this story. I was ashamed (3) because I jumped ship. This story had a reason I was ashamed of. I was fed up with being alone in Paris and I found my life dull. If there hadn't been that Hitler business. He was a great Zionist. Perhaps I thought it was better to be two against Hitler but I don't remember.

As for you, where's the shame for what you put up with from this Gregor guy? I ought to have told you about Wertheimer's fly. A twenty-five-year-old who shows you a hole in his jaw and who only stops trembling in order to vibrate, I eliminate. You didn't know how and you believed. Another kind of sickness. The first day I ought to have said: Not one Cent! *I put my foot!*

I wonder who could tell me why you didn't.

—*Whereas I, I was thinking, the things I shouldn't have put up with I thought it was my duty to put up with.*

All it took was one thing for me to keep going. A guy who coughs a little: disgusted I force myself not to refuse, I say.

I WON'T WRITE THIS BOOK

I'd have had to stop listening to the Vroom Vroom chant of the iron lung had I wanted to be able to get back together with my mother on the banks of the account book and take a train the other way with her, I'd have had to make up my mind on the spur of the moment to leap from the taxi the plane the lung, but I was under the Vroom Vroom charm, I wasn't Ulysses, I couldn't resist the chorus of the dead Georges, George George and Gregor I was stuck stock still under the table on the rim of the black gulf in a tangle of telephone and tape recorder wires, this business of listening to the snoring of iron machines was brimful of desperate pain. The charmed is aware he is charmed. The lung patient is aware he is charmed. Within the vault of his own chest a battle rages out of control between his strengths and his weaknesses in the morning victory at lunch retreat, the inner adversaries turn the lung patient into a puppet now on the point of death, now resuscitated so as to die again. The charmed person knows and cannot break the charm, his fate is in the grip of demons D, N, and A, D, A, N, short for damnation. Vroom Vroom says my mother.

So now here we are in the *Vroom Vroom period*, those vulgar sounds that would once have made me protest, offended, no longer touch me in the least but partake of my mother's brute charm, her environment, her free trade zone, her country, not extending beyond the desk lamp's halo.

It's not that I've become indifferent again, I was thinking, it's that I discover a completely different version of this story on the opposite bank, in Vroom Vroom land the comic version of Homer in which as my mother tells it Aeschylus was a soldier sailor capable of anything not in the least like his father nor like my father and who comes back alive after a long voyage in the opposite direction to ours.

And yet, I was thinking, I won't write this book. Such exhaustion overcomes me steals my blood and my light makes me sink to the ground

I won't write this book, once again chaos has invaded my study with a fury increased by the calm of these past few days, it's true I have managed to rewrite a few fragments that clasp hands like children, but several times I've also written little off-shoots of tales, tales off to the side, played hooky, I am scratched all over I couldn't stop myself, ten times a day I go down to the garden I shake off my study I let myself go on the pretext of helping my mother plant a camellia though I know I am digging my grave under the oaks secretly I weep dry tears I want to write this book it doesn't want, and when I don't want any longer it wants I can see what is happening but I have an-other brain in my head, another brain in my brain when I go down immediately the delicious garden turns to graveyard I rush back up I'd still prefer to die upstairs the marble staircase has become a vertical labyrinth upstairs might be as low as I get

You stayed locked up for months says my brother without ever coming out of your study what's she doing up there doing nothing said my grandmother every day I never see her I set the tray down outside her closed door Omi used to tell me says my brother you can't imagine what that meant, Omi completely locked out my grandmother in the incurable exclusion that had struck every part of the house.—I was alone I say with the chil-dren beside me—You were alone with Omi locked up in the walls of your locking-out which was even harder for Omi not to be hers but yours—I am frightened too late I say frightened and dreadfully sad to have locked Omi up in such lockings-up to have forgotten her and shut her up in the house outside my closed door, and then to have forgotten right up until my brother disinters her how I had for months forgotten all about her, and then after that how I locked the forgetting of her up inside another forgetting right to the Utter Forgetting of Omi. Yet I remember having forgotten the world and the universe the countries with their wars but I absolutely do not remember the utter forgetting of Omi and I too no longer know what she was doing up there doing nothing month after month what the grandmother is doing downstairs or even if she is there she hasn't a care or worry or any news being locked up in her own world it doesn't interest her in the least to know how life goes on "down there" in the house "here" being in the USA.

I wove spiderweb letters—from the top of the donjon I kept my ear tuned to the mailman's motor, I had two children filed away in the bedrooms next to the study, where I took myself to be their mother and so they could be my children I had two children for mothers, Omi who made the meals has gone, one after another I told them Shakespeare's plays which they told me back in anger and changing the truth, you climb up to the top you change your nature I never went downstairs I was terrified of having to creep down the labyrinth between the study and earth miles of passageways tiled with mortuary tiles one becomes an idea of a bird one tries to think going after the thoughts that come up one presses against the shadow of a thought, turn back we think a keep-your-back-straight kind of thought, and right away no no whatever you do don't turn back Monday I was scared at the idea of following my thought right to the end, I'll follow it Tuesday I thought Wednesday at the latest I followed my thought keeping close to it in the hallway, suddenly blackness, the light cut off I backtracked the next day I took off faster almost running pushing on ahead toward the target suddenly the lights go out, I scared myself with my fear, I forbade it to speak, I put a gag on its whispers I put a knife to its throat: I fell silent. Quiet! *For Gregor's sake hold your tongue!* This mute dread is not unfamiliar. I lived with it in the idiotic shut-up silences of my childhood. We kept company right to the age of nine, in the underground in the labyrinths in the hollows under orderly society. I lived with it huddled up in the great terror of childhood. You are an insect lost in the gigantic City with its gigantic distances from one street to the next yawning abysses, from the door of the classroom to the infirmary you can't even measure the space it is so vague and indescribable, a dead forest the ruins of a city bombarded by time. No point anywhere is accessible. It's a mistake to look out the windows giant heads sway there without bodies, they are giant-heads, one look and, seen, they think they've been invited in, received. Your mental sufferings are so great you can't tell anyone, not even yourself they are bigger than your mouth bigger than your brain bigger than your father bigger than god. Around you the others are fine.

You are going to dwindle to death. Every day suffering and global disproportion pare you down. You get further and further away from any kind of understanding, any hope of help. You understand nothing that would understand you, all this is your personal destiny, you are that consumptive illness described by Grimm and others, the others are fine, you are fading away you'll never have the courage to say anything, if you could talk about it, that would imply healing, opening of the vital orifices, but you have neither door nor mouth, from your throat would come caws of crows better to die without having betrayed the secret that kills. Ever since childhood it's always this question that leaps up and cannot come down again, it flees moaning with anguish ahead of the answer and finally it lets itself drop into the sea remain silent how long? When stop falling silent? Will it ever come, the messianic day I can say what I can't say without dying and which kills me, and survive, when will it be the day I can kill the silence that is killing me, when will there be a when that doesn't drop like a stone into the sea? In the shrunken heights there is neither truth nor lies there is

When did I begin to know? No no there was no beginning there was no knowing I never knew one can't know such things they would drive us mad when one begins to fear beginning to fear beginning to know no no, and that bitter word, the most bitter of all, the word suspicion, suspicion, oh that word with big gray ears that drag on the ground alongside its little ratmouse body that horrid shy fearful word that flings itself under my legs I stagger and fall from the top of the stairs down to the bottom, a touch of dizziness, it's the staircase that has suddenly forked, this happens to me regularly from time to time the world is joined by its own double the underworld seeps out of the world and takes its place to the right of the world under my eyes it's clear though a little murky everything has an omnipotence-other at its side to each its other or its shadow suddenly oh my god my godevil mycat grows a second mycat just when I was about to take it the staircase adds a flight stretched out to the right of the same staircase and my foot forks underfoot.

And if he didn't exist and if he didn't exist and if he existed then I would I wouldn't would I be I? Are you feeling better? You yes but what about You off to the side? I should have taken the one on the side, the side on the side. But in the torrents of light from the depths of time that suddenly flood the stairwell the side always wavers and changes sides, which is the real side of the side and I fall. The eye, the eye but the eye, the double of the hidden eye that sees in the back of my head, hides it, in the wink of an eye, where is its double, who is its double?

In vain the trees thrust a flock of winds at the windows, here all we see are the long streets with their storeyed buildings guarded by New York doormen.

Now in the little room besieged from within is the Apparition of a Horrid Thought sometimes it just squats in the telephone to which it gives the shape of a spidercorpse with vile paws and corkscrew tail. Sometimes it takes to whispering, it is a letter about to go off and torpedo a crazy boat residing under a false name in some apartment on Riverside Drive. On all the walls ant processions fall into line beside the Horrid Thought.

But all I need is to look at the little i.d. photo in which the suspect calmly smiles to convince me the madness is mine.

Why not believe the unbelievable?

After my two months' silence, in May I stepped out onto the balcony. I could see that everything shone with lighter shadow and I began to write to the most famous of his friends you can't allow a young intellectual to be arrested for spying without anyone doing a thing about it, he can't be effaced from the world like a dream whatever his strength his talents his degrees his promises during the night might have been. He was a musician as well, beloved by Klemperer. And his book? The Book of Imitations? Where has it gone? What are his friends the great American intellects, masters of physics and atomic energy doing?

"Dear Professor Nobel Prize in Physics P. Kusch of Columbia University."

There.

—All the same it went on for a quite while says my mother. A few weeks. Six millions already.

—A lot longer than that I say.

—I say "a few months" and my words stun me. Those few months lasted a hell, a bouquet of heartache roses, bunches of red-hot swords. They lasted the other life, a death and its tragic surroundings three or four deathbed agonies, each eternity three seasons long. And all that made a revolution, a round century, a complete turn of the mental dial.

And all that is a musical form: a *Dies Irae*
Vroom Vroom Vroom Vroom says my mother.

A TRAGIC END

Fleeing, the scholars have arrived at the top of the City ramparts
along with their guide or protector a young man, the hero, the
one who has just disappeared into the depths of the pitch-black
abyss. Did he dive? Did he fall? It seems to me he had a rope to
start. Or maybe he wanted to look for something at the bottom
of the water? The dreamer stands below on the edge of the pit.
Suddenly, catastrophe. The hero is drowning. He flails as if he
were trapped at the bottom, you see nothing but eddies and
bubbles shimmering in rings on the black surface of the crater,
you can hear him calling underwater, but the water swallows
his shouts, weeping almost. And those above do nothing? Nobody dives into the black water to try to save him? He's still
alive, bubble message, no one, frail bubbles on the black water.
The dreamer who has no power over this scene bends to the
murky water and dips her useless hand pitifully into the black
aware that if by some miracle in which she doesn't believe the
hero floated up close enough to grab her hand he would grab
an insubstantial hand incapable of pulling him out. But plunging her arm into the water she grasps the horror of the scene.
Black, syrupy, filled with large black leaves and dense shadowy
weeds that must have imprisoned and trapped the person
unlucky enough to have ventured in, the blind water is not
water but a sticky, murderous omnipotence-other. With their
strength, some ropes, those from the City above ought to have
tried? Did they give up right away discouraged by the hopeless-
ness of the task? Did they give up earlier? Yet, when the first
airy rings of beads on the dark funnel cried out, he must still
have been findable.

Atrocious groan of farewell. Black duration of a minute drowned.

Whereas the "death" of Gregor cannot be compared to any other death. "Death" is not the word. There was no agony, at least visible. A ring of beads, perhaps, on a night? The "death" had no time, at least not for me. The place? No one knows exactly. All New York perhaps was suddenly covered in a black mist.

The announcement of his "disappearance" ("disappearance" is not the word. Annulment? Dissolution, maybe) was Kusch's letter. Wake up. The play is over.

All the actors have gone home to bed. *The world's last night is done.* The curtain has fallen.

Say how terrifying the expression "it was a dream" is when it designates a figment of reality. A crack in the garden. Thought fissured from top to bottom. An axe blow splits the skull right to the forehead. It's not deadly but it might as well be. The house full of thick black water full of stuck-together leaves. Yesterday there was a hero under this roof, nothingness has swallowed him up.

The pain is left. Which? The double of my life. The passions. The embers are not cold but they are without a hearth. From one moment to the next, end of the addressee, he has neither left, nor died, he is no longer on this earth, he never was.

Left: Pain Dread Love Fear. They entered the Beinecke Library, they took their place in the flesh of my memory, for their set they built New York as interim representative they took a character as fictionally strong, of an imaginary substance as unreal as Gregor Samsa. Once the play is done, the lights back on you understand all of a sudden that the true immovable characters, the immortals, are those faceless powers Love Fear Death Suffering.

* * *

Suddenly, without warning, he was no longer there to love. For a while I felt like a hand stretched out in a dream toward the hand held up from under the layers of mud. Then: no one.

I laughed a lot. I was sitting on the front steps of the house and looking at the empty stage I was laughing. I shed the other version of tears.

ELPENOR'S DREAM

—*I've never wanted to be Kafka,* or Stendhal, I tell myself and I make a list of all the people whom I might out of love have wished to be, practically all writers I noted, letting the faces of those who greatly please me come to mind, first of all I invoked Montaigne, then all the ones I love whom I could never have wished to be, Freud, for instance, I've never wanted to be Rousseau; I set aside Rimbaud; I've never wanted to be those without whom I don't exist, and with whom I maintain a kind of complicity nourished by special secret deeds that send a kind of mental and linguistic intoxication coursing through my entire being, I've never wanted to be any of my vital beings not François Villon nor Selma Lagerlöf nor Dostoyevsky nor Derrida; I set Blanchot whom I love intensely with a repulsion like the repulsion that is part and parcel of my great complicity with Poe to one side, I've never felt the deadly aberration of those who are unhappy with themselves I've never wanted to be a painter or a musician, when at the age of twelve I wanted to be a doctor so as to reincarnate my doctor father right away I sensed that I was on the verge of suicide, before everyone I proclaimed that I wanted to be a doctor and I promptly saw myself as a horrified doctor, disgusted by the blood, a suicide doctor an assassin of patients, here I am in the guise of a doctor, doctor medical monkey, as if I could have brought my father back to life by slipping into his professional skin, a music hall idea, I've never wanted to be a doctor, I've never wanted to be my father I tell myself frightened by my own sacrilegious feather-headedness, a crime against medicine, a crime against truth, a crime against life's chances, a crime against myself first victim of my own blather. I myself had been lying to myself. Luckily I didn't believe myself. Before the year was out I unmasked myself, I announced that for nothing in the world would I become a doctor, sick people scare me I say, I fear the exaltation of sick people, I fear bodies whose every orifice starts talking, who hear the voices of their organs, of their blood, of all the canals, arteries, streets, internal monuments. I didn't need to be other others. My own others were just fine. My brother signed up for medicine and my mother's father for the German army. In literature there are no uniforms I thought.

In the chill April sun I was now sitting with my brother the doctor rescued from medicine, a one-in-a-million thing I tell myself, and all the more unique I tell myself, in having wended his way for thirty-eight years in a direction opposite to himself and therefore having managed to pull the wool over his own eyes he says uninterruptedly for at least thirty-seven years, thereupon having managed to find his own direction again without this revolution having ruptured any vital organ while my brother was turning his life in the opposite direction, a maneuver whose first fruits, given the huge weight of the ship, took months, each day I feared the coronary, my brother is a one hundred percent successful case of someone turning himself inside out, I know who I'm talking to I tell myself, at least I think I do.

—He would have liked to be Kafka I say but I didn't even know then thirty years ago there are people around who want to be others completely and utterly; or rather he wanted to be Kafka, instead of being *a* Kafka which he could have been I say. I love literature above all, this always gives my thinking process a dangerous simplicity, thought without hesitation can never imagine how thought with hesitation works my mother also has never understood anyone, most people are not capable of parking in front of the store they need to run an errand in, the others dither interminably before always finding a place too far from where they wish to be whereas I always know exactly where I'm going she says and I find the exact perfect spot as planned, says my mother who comes to us in the first flush of her morning triumph. Going to the market is not just running errands. It's outsmarting all the good-for-nothings, the slow-pokes, the can't-make-up-their-minds, the confused, and the panic-stricken who look as if they want to turn tail and run, flee, flee from something in the end, they flee themselves right up to the day they can't flee any further. The earth has limits after all. Why would anyone want to be Kafka says my mother, what a strange idea Kafka had no luck unfortunately he had that handicap yourfather too a shame since he was a go-getter he couldn't sleep, he was miserable not to have slept on the one hand he was miserable not to have slept, plus fearing his insomnia he brought it on, it was all he could think of, into the bargain he'd get even more upset at not having slept, which during the day fed his fear of not being able to sleep that night, this problem of not being able to stop not being able to think about his insomnia, diminished him, health is a big thing, half of genius is good health, on the Osnabrück side people were hale but without a lick of genius, on the Prague side Kafka was half a genius for his ill health in Algeria there was tuberculosis and incest, I went across the street from the station and got some lamb for this evening says my mother, life being brief time is of the essence you have to do many things at once, some people can't do one even, they run they run they run they need to make themselves miserable, do you see? she tells me whereupon she leaps back up on her invisible charger called Indignation and without wasting a second's energy, heads for the kitchen, her philosophical laboratory.

He wanted to be Kafka and thus flee Gregor, I was thinking, therefore he didn't absolutely want to be Kafka, he wanted both to rid himself of Gregor *and* be Kafka. Except for the name. Or maybe he would have liked a certain Kafka to be him, Gregor. He would have liked to be a great writer of fables, allegories I say and I've always thought that he had almost been that, I always thought he had genius I say and after the end of the affair I could still believe he had genius misplaced unfortunately he himself didn't realize this although he wanted it at whatever price he had taken himself for someone else entirely to the complete and utter ruin of his own identities. Had he written down that story he concocted day after day in order to make believe he was a real writer he would have been a real writer I say perhaps I say I'm not sure of anything.

All of a sudden sitting across from me in the Beinecke Library, he had been overcome by the need for fable, or so I imagine. I imagine he was possessed. You see that in Shakespeare in the Greeks. You are sitting at the edge of the temple terrace. The spirit of a god or spirit flits by and suddenly the landscape you were contemplating without noticing it starts to shimmer, it wakes it wakes you and you see that you are not a subject sitting in a chair on the edge of world's set but that the world is happening to you.

You too my brother says you are one of those caught in the clutches of fable, you have always favored the intellectual capacities you don't know the earth, your measure is literary, you didn't know the farm with its beams blackened by the fire of time, you don't know the hundred-year-old vineyard you didn't see the June storm whose egg-sized hailstones in a minute massacre a lifetime's work, you don't know the memory that goes on living in the earth, your memory is literary, in the springtime you didn't see a cow standing in all its glory without glory at the far end of the empty field with its nose in a hawthorn bush you can't look at a cow standing on its four legs without turning it into a literary cow, you don't know the cow standing said my brother in his slow melodious voice neither reproach nor accusation, I listened enchanted thinking: it's all in the tone, the same sentences pronounced in a scandalized tone of voice would be directed against me but they weren't how, I thought, enchanted and perplexed, how to render in writing the gentleness of a grief-stricken voice, it's always a matter of the voice and the tone I was thinking, the page lacks its musical notation here I should indicate: "Song of my brother to the Cow Standing On Its Four Legs, himself lowing in the bush, himself the Cow Standing at the far end of the field, himself caught in the grips of the vision and the fable."

—He could have been a writer, an other, someone that is who would have been one of his own selves, or someone who would have been himself, but perhaps that was impossible for him not being anyone perhaps in his own eyes he could only want an other in place of himself, I imagine him coming along to pick a self off the mirrory shelves of the great Beinecke department store, an author to suit him evidently. Drawn by more than one, undecided, seduced soon captivated, but needing advice for the final choice.

What a mistake, but inescapable, not to have believed in himself (whoever this was) in the presence of a self as good as the next and to have become a robber of souls. A genius of a robber. You can tell the genius by *what* he steals. *That* he steals. By his flights of fancy. An idiot thief: he should have flown on his own, robbed himself, had he known. Instead of going to take his self from an other, risk everything in a rickety calculation, be just a montage about to collapse.

Or did he live in a jealous youthful naïveté, there he is copying the soul of men older than himself, as if he were the young widower in mourning for himself?

Or maybe none of those violent events which bring about the birth of a soul dedicated to the literary alliance had ever happened to him yet, none of those circumcisions of a part of the spiritual body none of those cuts in the shape of mouths which open to writing's first imprecations he had never yet lost a father perhaps or the friend dearer than himself, or brother or little child or the poor Lambert who brought the little Henri Brulard into the world by tumbling out of the mulberry tree and spilling all his blood into a little chipped faience basin, the basin too wounded and circumcised, sometimes the terrible suffering of a beloved dog is all it takes to trace a crack in the heart. Other kinds of uprooting exist. But some people reach their thirtieth, fortieth year, spared and hence grievously deprived of the spear thrust and its wound. I imagine he had the misfortune to have not yet been visited by misfortune.

Whereas I had already had *negative luck*, I had lost my father early on and after that the dog my father's son and right after almost that I'd had to leave my own son on the threshold, and each time losing them once again in each of them losing the others all over again I saw destiny as war, like a besieged city I awaited the next misfortune, I had dug a shelter in under my life and stocked it with books, let each in himself see his own salvation, for a long time I had known that this world is a prison I'd managed to slip my own freedom into it I believed, he probably didn't, I believe.

In my opinion I say he had not yet lost anything except for right reason but you never lose reason you only exchange it for one equally but differently twisted. And in his haste to become, instead of awaiting a good blow he had borrowed I imagine I say, running his eye along the shelves and consulting the prefaces and time lines of those elected by misfortune, I imagine, from this one his sick lungs from another the death of his mother on the day of his birth, making short shrift of his biography, I am imagining the method of his self-portraiture, but you could imagine quite the contrary: a cataclysm or a war, that deprived him of fathermotherbrothers and left him naked and without any witness for himself, his self too might well have been buried in the quake.

He believed himself, I say, I see no other explanation, he believed himself the exact same. The idea of becoming the same in the fastest and most direct manner was to send me the raw cooked-up incredible Letter post-haste. Here's the trap: The Letter. Having copied it out in its entirety. The Letter goes off, travels for two days. For two days you know nothing of it. It arrives. Whereupon the trap works I say, unfortunately for him I was thinking but maybe he thought the opposite, it took me in it clapped shut over me therefore over him, the way the trap worked I was saying was beyond calculation.

All my fault I say, I think this for the first time thirty-five years after the fact, I say. He had marvelous bad luck meeting up with me of all people, me with my literary and symbolic hypersensitivity to the pulmonary region. Lungs, cough, hospitals, this is what I fear, this is what is dear to me. Add to this all of Literature. "Oh the poor usurper of breaths, poor dreamer of crowns." These words come to me for the first time thirty-five years after the fact, I noted. I sigh for the fate of the wretched painter of scars I tell myself and for the first time I hear myself sigh for the fate of the trapeze-artist imposter.

It was all my fault: I loved Literature above all and I hadn't read *Letters to Milena*. And *who* hasn't read *Letters to Milena*? I was already an academic. Where does imposture start? Responsibility, irresponsibility? Responsibility half-blind?

On the one hand as soon as I read his lines I no longer had the least doubt of his genius. It hit you in the eye. Blindness, enucleation, dust, speck of glass in the eye this is what I dread, this is what dazzles me.

I am happy sitting to the left of my brother on the earth's southern slope; up above, the visible: soft blue light through the palms of the oak; down below the invisible: German voices mingling in the kitchen, the hundred year old voices:—*Sollen wir die Schlüßel hier lassen—Ja die Schlüßel läßt man immer hier*. Between the two scenes the whole space of time, my mother is still living I owe her forever the monstrous phone bill and all the beauty of the world is the dream on the face of my beloved, I was thinking. Between the two languages all of time's dream and it all happened in an omnipotence-other language.

So I need this great stretch of happiness, this enduringness with its roots thrusting their fingers down to the center of the earth in order to attempt at last the ascension of Mount Dread, thirty-five years later I heave myself out of my paralysis in order to attain the point of compassion.

With these high winds I've so hurried that here I am at last in pity's doorway.

—Or maybe he was a poor wretch of a human being avid to the point of folly for liberty he wanted the dream to come true:

descend from neither father nor mother nor historical memory, be the author of an authorless young man even just for a day, perhaps dream a short week away, let's say some kind of unlimited eternity—the time of an elevator trip from false to true,

(I was thinking: a white bird like a sugar lump of light has just settled on a bough of a pine or maybe it's the hand of an angel on time's shoulder, I don't know how I know: this punctuation is meant for me, I need it seems all these signals from on high to scale Mount Dread today)

and unfortunately by chance in the elevator he meets someone who takes him literally, to the letter G and that's it for his liberty now he has to G to Ge he has to go along has to play the game.

The player could have lost from the very first round. Or the second. And like any completely ruined player he would have been spared the anguish that goes with the process of losing. Unfortunately for him, he got lucky. So each round he won in fact upped his losses.

He who entered my bloodstream via the injection of the secret name who other than some omnipotence-other had given him the key to my tomb?

I know nothing of the character who was playing the role of G.

Is the actor more or less real than the real person?

The character was acted for eight months. Then the actor brings the performances to a halt and instantly the character is torn to bits and tossed in the bin.

But this character would never have existed had I not believed him to the quick, cruel credulousness. To be Kafka for weeks on end was no doubt exalting but then to be him still and for a long time deadly exhausting. On the one hand I made him: he "played" "Kafka" and unaware of what I was in reality doing I applauded him, praised him to the skies, I took him *literally*, and he was done.

This Unknown to me whom I believed I knew, this shade I took for a young man, what sort of Disconsolate Person might he have been? He who didn't want himself, didn't love himself, but loved Literature above all, to the point of the suppression of himself? A looter of artworks, a fool of a hunter upon whom the hunt might at any moment turn?

But this kind of hunter most likely only expects a passing prey, the shadow of a prey, a minuscule eternity. The mask is made for a day. After a few days it brings on allergies, bruises. Now look what comes along, out of the blue, a prey without a shadow of flight.

All these pointless ideas about someone who lasted eight months apparently, but who never was, except in appearance, short of breath, crowded into the garden now. I am astounded by the wealth of uncertainties simmering there where once the whole story could be contained in the narrow little cage of Room 91.

It's not that "I no longer loved him" it's that I had only ever loved the shadow of a book dressed up in a young man's body and, the book having gone back to its origin, he had vanished in between the volumes.

Now I remembered the scene of judgment on January 1, 1965, and I marveled at its secrets, which I had never suspected. "Look, look, I feel a hidden presence, there is someone else here with us, find the keys, the keys." And rendered blind by the one-eyed character I looked looked literally in my own drawers, for what was not in the drawers.

—He never got back in touch, the schizophrenic?

—More different even more unimaginable than what I imagine perhaps guiltier or more concerned shiftier more of a criminal or a whole lot stranger mentally and perhaps given to attacks of simulated life, life as a sort of epilepsy which, when the attack is over, leaves not a trace of a memory. Perhaps I never existed for the usurped man save in a quite long but rather brief dream, when he awoke in a flash he was back at his old life at his own address and under his own name which was not in truth Gregor. Could he have been an Elpenor? Also a strangely slim life.—El-penor?—That doesn't mean anything to you? I say—Not a thing, *que dal,* says my brother. I don't get it.

Elpenor Queudal Elpenor Not a Thing I was thinking, we couldn't in vain have found a better name for such a resonant character.

A sense of pure mortality, long death short life I say, a nobody I say, the sidekick of another, one of Ulysses' companions, Nobody in Person a part of the Whole, a mere buckle on the belt of the greatest of heroes, the-one-who-didn't-have-time, the absolute stand-in for the tragedy of mortals—Elpenor, a junior mortal. Look at Elpenor I say his whole history escaped him forever, does he have a mother, did he have a father, he is nothing he knows nothing, he has no childhood, no deeds high or low, nothing ever happened to him, one Elpenor nobody notices the youngest of us all, doesn't listen to advice, a not-yet-and-maybe-never, and that's him, this person, this Mr Vague, this nothing at all to whom in a flash all of death happens, everyone else has just been set free, for the twenty-two companions who have just stopped being pigs and the twenty-two non-pigs, a new lease on life, at which point, one of them a nobody sets himself up as the hero of zero, a bolt from the blue illustration of the fragility of us all.

How does death come? Where? By what means? I am going to tell you says Homer I say. Here you have Mister Sir Vague who, besotted with wine, just happens to nod off on the terrace of Circe's temple. When the forty-four men arise the hubbub of the voices and the bird song wakes him. He jumps up says Homer and forgets everything says he, and so with Gregor, I say *first he jumps awake next he forgets everything:* he wakes up and that's when he no longer knows who he is where he is.

Look at Elpenor I say he nods off on the edge of the neighbor's roof, and while he sleeps he is someone in a dream, a famous man, the great writer, in the crowd around him you can make out the actors the directors the young academics still full of ambition, the philosophers, and him, he who delivers a passionate lecture, an evocation of great biblical characters, riding the wave of his own success he mixes up everything, in any case he himself is all mixed up, he takes the part of King Moses, at one moment he strides into the den of a cave and he shouts very loud old Lazarus! Come on up out of there! Up comes Lazarus. People in the room don't agree. Lazarus? says a young philosopher. Not born yet! The purists rightly sneer. But I realize art scoffs at history's order. What counts is to bring to life, breathe spirit into, rouse up, fie on verisimilitude, have anyone you like, thanks to the power of the name. Lazarus! shouts the king: up comes Lazarus. This is what Elpenor Gregor sees in his dream. I myself go up to him in the dream, one of the crowd and I tell him: Gregor that was magnificent!

I am the King he tells me sharply. The King—I say on stage, of course. *I am the King* he asserts with authority. If you like I say, thinking that directors of genius sometimes extend imagination's domain right into the fields of reality. In any case me, I am me I tell myself. And since I am right beside him I see with some astonishment that he has made up his eyes, delicately but still, having outlined them with kohl, this gives him a mask for a face that he pretends is his real face which has finally returned to power after a long time somewhere else. This simple artifice gives him youth immemorial and a sort of massiveness as well, head big as a statue nostrils flaring, a mere mask makes the king I tell myself impressed by these sleights of hand. Naturally I renounce the idea of speaking up for reality what's the point? I am delighted to see King Moses and Lazarus stir up trouble in this academic crowd. He leaps up and forgets everything. I on the other hand leap up and make haste to write down the dream that is slipping away.—An absurd dream, I say, wild, swathed in veils, why bother saving it, let's not be as absurd awake as in the dream, right, *write* I say, write down the scene that *wants* to escape from you—watch out for yourself Circe would have you forget, it is your duty as living being to disobey the strange advice instilled in your brain. Write or lose the memory of your own being. I write. He forgets everything. Instead of going to take the great spiral staircase down into the garden where my brother and I sit looking East, he goes straight, crosses the invisible border, falls off the roof, breaks his neck, and his soul descends to the dead like a stone on your back, dead, legs stretched toward the lost sky. Now nobody had heard of Elpenor before his death I say. See Elpenor and you see Gregor. People whose whole life is caused by one strike of death. Before death they don't exist, they are the companions of a great poet, *graduate* students. But on the other hand they dream. All day of the dream they race around the disorderly cities, they reign over roomfuls of subjects from all walks of life whom they charm with their extraordinary inventions of superhuman events, if they feel like it they pass for Homer, effortlessly, even if one part of the chorus is against them, and as long as the Sun of the Dream sheds its light on the world everything goes swimmingly. It's at the moment of waking that Danger lurks: the dream's sun has set, so to forget *everything*, forget on both sides, forget your memory of the coast your sense of earth and sea, forget your sense of the *passage* which ensures immortality with one bound instead of going back down as you must taking the detour of the great twisting staircase, for from life to death and vice versa it is necessary to *take the spiral staircase,* this bit of time in a spiral that allows the dreamer to voyage from one side to the other by degrees so as to be sure to keep separate and whole the two universal kingdoms that can only be inhabited one after the other, the person who wishes to inhabit both lives must at all cost avoid the risk of confusion, one leap and you break the neck of the dream, instead of coming back to earth in stages, Elpenor Queudal goes straight ahead and falls off the roof to the dead. This makes a thud like the body of a squirrel falling from the mast of a pine. Thud, dead, clean break. Between dream and death the slender space of a step. A death without death in a time without reason, an unmixed death, from this pure event the character of Elpenor the unknown man will be born. Look look says my brother look at the ones who never die, we were watching the squirrels, who were racing up and down the great staircases of the trees, and in the fountain of sun coursing down the long and once again young and gold branches of the oaks, you could almost hear the brief rustle of the drop from a roof.

—Did he cry out? thinks my brother.—Apparently not. Nobody said anything. If he shouted it was for no one.

Now had he not been dead of dead of having taken death for life, nothing nothing at all would be left of Elpenor, the whole of his history, his existence, his sexual life, his professional prospects, about which we know nothing, come down to the flash of genius of his faux pas, his false step: instead of heading for life like the rest of them that day without the least hesitation he goes in the opposite direction, he thinks he's going right he plunges left, there he is at last with his tribe dead with the dead, having not had a life he returns to oblivion, at last he is a real shadow after having dragged around for years wrong way out acting the part of a false shadow of a great writer; alive and a fake everybody forgot about him, he himself was forever forgetting his own memory. What a relief to discover the exit that spares him a wretched existence. One step, and he's off. He never did anything all by himself, on his own, except take this step.

Gregor Elpenor Queudal inventor of no-life, says my brother, not bad.

AFTER THE END

I had such love for Literature, therefore for him I thought, thirty-five years after Gregor's exit, the idea comes to me of the suffering he had sown for himself, I loved literature and believed he was it, whereas he knew he had borrowed it, he knew I didn't know my love wasn't love for him, I feared his death as the end of Literature, he knew that my love would outlive his poor borrowed persona, I'd never loved him, he knew, the idea comes to me only after having been able to delight in the fruit of his textual pillages and in the success of his spell-casting for a while, he must have begun to suffer from my blindness, I didn't see *him*, I didn't admire *his* art, now he's the one who is spellbound now he is the conjured object. I loved him for his counterfeit genius he would have liked to be loved for his other genius the counterfeiting genius.

Perhaps, in part two of the play, his ferocity, his rage, because I had caught him in the trap he had set? And now locked up in

Kafka's skin with Donne's tongue in his mouth, in what form how would he get out?

Changed into a crow, bound hand and foot in the tale of a madman? Like a turtle dangling live by one leg on the tale-teller's stall?

I had the strength to wait months for him, I had the strength to take a plane in a storm, I had the strength to go to the CIA, to the Office of the President of the United States, I alerted the International Human Rights Commission. He was surrounded persecuted by his own inventions, arrested, suspected of spying, at his wits' end in the labyrinth that had turned against him and desperately seeking an exit.

He must be leafing through Poe, Balzac, Dostoyevsky, looking for models of extravagant chapters, you can find whatever you want in Literature but it's tiring.

Beginning with the Scar scene, he's someone else.

Think about the Scar as the border between two tales, two worlds, Perhaps as the final stroke.

If he conceived of the scenario, the Scar is ingenious, brilliant, ingeniously undecidable, brilliantly undecidably ingenious: Should I "not have seen it"? Or "see" it. See that it was "false." Perhaps he held it out to me with a beggar's hand *to read*, like an avowal? Which of the two characters is the blind, the mad, the one-eyed one. Say here that there exists a kind of disturbance called "from-the-double-point-of-view": one can not see what one sees for one only sees what one believes one sees; one cannot see what one sees for one only sees what one wants to see; one believes one sees what one does not see for one only sees what one believes. What had I seen? What had I refused (1) to see (2) not to see? What does he think that I don't think? Would he have wanted feared wantedfeared to see himself not to see himself stripped of all his masks at once? He has more and more of them. Or is each mask destined to mask the other masks?

Was the idea of doubling it up with Patch, the eye-cover, a good idea? This remains to be seen.

Or the contrary? He gets himself ever deeper into the mounting madness.

And I have the force to follow him. But now we were at the Summit of Simulation. Where to keep on to? At the end of the play you must come up with *the* scene that puts an end to the unending.

For him there is no way out but a prison scene, acted from behind the curtain. Better than Orestes' temple to flee the Eryinyes.

There, nowhere, I lose all track of him.

In the last scene, instead of Room 91 of the King's Crown Hotel, instead of the never-set-eyes-on Hospital room, solitary imprisonment in a cell for reasons of State Security, no name of a prison. In this sequence you see me open an enormous but vague door. And not another word. Instead of sentences which ought to have followed a gravelly voice fills my chest.

—"Radio-Mystery here," says my brother doyouremember? In a flash I fall back terrified with my brother in the great big brown leather armchair that floats in front of the radio in Algiers in 1948 after the shipwreck of my father.

Radio-Mystery here booms the favorite voice of our Algerian radiophonic terrors.

"Well, well, well," said the Mystery, said my brother and I together.

"Vroom vroom" says my mother.

(Insert somewhere in this suite of ends, when I speak of the Scar scene: It is here and on that very day, January 1, 1965, I see

him in "reality" for the final last time and forever. At the time I haven't a clue. What about him? Does he make up his mind it is to be so that night? Before? After? Is "the last time" already stamped with its name on the last room of The King's Crown Hotel? Or is it "the last night of the world"?

Must we consider (interpret) the Scar scene as a cortege comprising: Room 91, bouquet of red roses, black Patch—and perhaps snow storm as well, as a vroom-vroom equivalent of the famous scene of the Fisher King, impotent lord of a devastated land in The Grail Story, set in the castle (= King's Crown Hotel), in which you see a spear with on its tip a bead of blood appear (Spear = 1) Roses? (2) the hand mine scratching the Scar on the sacred Body

a golden grail, a silver platter, an ivory chair (the toilet bowl as Socratic stool). The august character they serve is not in the play (= Kafka?). The tale reproaches Perceval grievously for having neither understood nor asked questions. Because of his ill-timed discretion everything is lost once and for all beginning with The Tale condemned to eternal incompletion.

The whole of this mysterious and fatal cortege could have been thought up: by Gregor; or by Christian de Troyes; or it could be one version of rite of the Grand Entry, with iconostasis (Greek Church), in the vroom-vroom version I would be either Lancea Christi or Perceval, thus either the cause guiltily innocent or more precisely the guiltinnocent cause of the irreparable or on the contrary the ignorant person who aspires from ignorance and thanks to ignorance, to a devotion and perfection that don't exist. How about the Grail? In my opinion this would have to be the Statue of Liberty which enflames America's mystical imagination, feeds its enthusiasm for allegory, and gives to each poor clown of an immigrant the idea of creating his own legend. Or maybe the blood-filled spittoon in the Intensive Care Unit of Vroom Vroom Hospital. Gregoros would be

*Jesus or the Fisher King (= King Fisher cf. Angus Fisher)
Brooklyn version, in either case shackled, paralyzed. Furthermore you will find this legend analyzed in* Allegory: The Theory
of a Symbolic Mode. *"Gregor" might have wished to borrow
and modify the mystical data so as to highlight their frightfully
marvelous side.)*

After the end I wore black. I was, all the same, bereft of myself.
I had lost a self and its strata of mysteries on the literature front.
A character quite the contrary to that of my mother whom I'd
always—right until I got to New York and even Buffalo—
allowed to rule me had risen up inside me. I myself had been a
character created by a character henceforth snuffed out but my
character continued to breathe inside me.

One side of my character had taken refuge inside me in the
place of my mother, the other part, which had lived through the
throes of the crime was now nothing but the memory of a role.
I had lost someone dear, I wanted to wear mourning. A bit of
plagiary, an act of piracy with two pirates.

But it might be Patch the eye-cover which grows into a black
flag and wraps itself around me.

During the duel someone is stabbed. You don't expect a
resurrection.

So I'm not just going back to my desk as if I hadn't lost (a)
death.

Year after year I attempt to paint myself as Scar but the
words are slippery. Three, four, five books hold me off.

After the end this story was all mine he'd made it up I'd
transformed it into a life with a deathbed scene.

I had lost my mind but gained madness where I'd never have
set foot had I known it was mad.

I had entered it in full sail as a great ship slides to port with
every stitch of its reason whipped in the wind.

He was deader than any dead person had ever been, dead with no survival dead of a death without life without any of those remains which continue to brood immortally, brought to life at the first puff of memory as the stir of moths in our clothes brings tears to our eyes. He had been dispersed without ashes without a sound. A soap bubble . . .

. . . never existed. Nothing of what happened had really happened.

I could not even observe his disappearance, there was no phenomenon.

I felt no curiosity. The earth was silent.

But with respect to myself the great violence of a fright. I was constantly fearful: I am a fool but perhaps this is false, I am two fools, for being one and for saying so. Everything that accompanies death was on my side. I might have been on a trip far from someone who might have been me. I might have spent thirty-five years in an airport knowing someone would never come back.

I did not approve of myself in the least and ever

I did wrong things at every instant everything *I* did could only be the wrong thing but it wasn't for me to say

I went around with a leper's rattle, I rattled myself

I was cracked I cracked open each gaze each and every vision that I saw each sentence that I said each word that I heard everything is maybe its opposite everything is opposite

everything: its contrary

I was saying I said to myself I say the contrary will be said

I had no subject any more

What remains are the objects (the imitation squirrel skin slippers thirty-five years asleep in the armoire, the fake crocodile suitcase on January 1, 1965) I didn't send them away

and the passions he left me with whereas their subject vanished completely having never existed

What remains is the City of New York in which I believed I had lived a life but it wasn't me and it wasn't her, but another person completely who'd come out of me in an omnipotence-other City come out of New York as a ghost city comes out of a real city being almost exactly the same thing, what remains is New York the theater in which the story I believed I lived acted itself out among the skyscrapers, on the corners of the avenues, steeping each instant and every site in a religious literary glory.

Above all I love the City of New York without inhabitants. The Dream of the Dream City for a film shoot

The events withdrew without any past outside history outside any story

What remains are the feelings and thoughts which stay around forever, not in the kitchen but in the trees or rather in the wind which gives them a soul and torment: risk, fear, broken faith, renunciation, the spiritual goods whose value is that they have no material value, their cost incalculable

everything my mother instinctively fights off

in ignorance of the war she is waging

of the siege and the military means of which ignorance itself is a part.

In the hands of her thoughts she clutches

the phone bill and the tin of pâté that are her compass points against shipwreck. Meanwhile dressed in black I fight for the inheritance of a mental cataclysm.

I no longer conceive of love without abandon without creative devastation without absolute creation of a virginity.

When I wanted to find the King's Crown Hotel

the building had totally vanished

In its place The Tale should commence.

I felt it was in the interest of this story, tale—*histoire, récit*—not to have footnotes, so as not to detract from its flow. These few, unnumbered notes are intended only as admission of the translation's most glaring failures. Elsewhere, to cope with Cixous's wealth of word play, if this did not feel clumsy, I have let French and English stand side by side, or resorted to two words or expressions in the place of her multifaceted one; for example, in the last chapter, to render the French *géniale* (page 232 in the original), which means having the quality of genius, in order not to lose the root *genius*, I used a combination of "ingenious" and "brilliant." I should also note that there are a number of places in the text where Hélène Cixous shifts between French and English; most of these shifts of language go unnoticed in my translation.

I would like to express my gratitude to the people who have read portions of this and other Cixous translations, and helped with their suggestions: Hélène Cixous, Eric Prenowitz, and Laurent Milesi.

PAGE VII, omnipotence-others: *Puissances-autres*. As Jacques Derrida posits in his book *Geneses, Genealogies, Genres and Genius* (Edinburgh: Edinburgh University Press, 2006) and in greater detail in his book *H.C. for Life, That Is to Say*, trans. Laurent Milesi (Stanford: Stanford University Press, 2006), the word *puissance*, as Cixous uses it, may be a combination of the subjunctive *puisse* ("may, might, let it") and the suffix *-ance*, and has a sense of potency; it should not, therefore, be translated, as "power/all-powerful." After consulting with Cixous and Laurent Milesi, I decided to translate *Puissance-autre* generally as "omnipotence-other," but occasionally as "almighty" or "all-powerful other."

PAGE IX, stealthy as wolves, on tiptoe like fools: *à pas de loups, à pas de fous*.

PAGE IX, We have eyes only for Him, this god: *Nous n'avons d'yeux que pour Lui*. Cixous plays on the homophony between *d'yeux* ("eyes") and *dieu* ("god") here and in the next paragraph.

CERTES A SACRIFICE

PAGE 10, It is certainly true that: *Certes*. *Certes* is purportedly the name of a place; it is also an adverb, meaning "certainly," and an anagram for the word *secret*.

PAGE 17. Ah! it cries: son!: *Ça crie: fils! Sacrifice!* The French *Ça crie: fils! ("It cries out: son!")* evokes the narrator's dead son but also the word *sacrifice*.

THE EYE-PATCH

PAGE 23, The Eye-Patch: *Le Cache-oeil*. This locution echoes and plays on the French idiom *cache-sexe* ("loincloth, G-string").

PAGE 24, I truly believed I'd seen in the raw. Believedsee: *j'ai bien cru voir cru*. *Cruvoir*. Cixous plays here on the homophony of the past participle of the verb *croire* ("to believe") and the adjective *cru* ("raw, uncooked").

PAGE 28, sighings and sufferings: *tous ces souffrirs*. In this unidiomatic turning of the verb *souffrir* ("to suffer") into a plural noun, one may also hear an echo of the noun *soupirs* ("sighs").

A YELLOW FOLDER

PAGE 39, NY on my own Secret NY—Ny of former days. N'y. Nie: *NY Secret NY—Ancien Ny. N'y. Nie.* Cixous plays here on various possible meanings and permutations of the letters N and Y: "New York," "deny" (*nier*), and the negation "not there" (*n'y*).

I WILL NOT WRITE THIS BOOK

PAGE 50, translate the words but not the tone: The first statement is in English in the original text; the second version is Cixous's translation of this into French. Cixous has modified the English, however, by changing, for example, "are working" into *se liguent* ("league together"), adding *vos mémoires* ("your memories") to the list, and making "out of date" the more forceful *nuls et péimés* ("null and void").

I AM NAKED

PAGE 95, Crude, the letter: *Une lettre crue. Crue* means both "crude" or "raw" and "believed" (verb *croire*). See note to page 24, above.

PAGE 96, into a reading lamp, a servant: *en servante (la femme, la lampe).* In French *une servante* may mean both a female servant and a free-standing reading lamp.

PAGE 101, You law law law loir: *Vous loi loi loi loir.* Cixous plays here with the words and sounds hidden inside *vouloir* ("to wish or want"); that is, *vous* ("you") and *loi* ("law").

THE CHARM OF THE MALADY

PAGE 111, John Donne: Cixous plays in this section of the text on the homonymy between the name of the English poet, quoting lines from some of his poems, and the French verb *donne* ("give").

The line of Donne's poem "Licence my roving hands" thus becomes in French translation in the original text "Donne à mes mains licence." and Dido's (*Didon*) love for Aeneas is echoed in the French of "dit Donne Donne Didon."

FOLLY USA

PAGE 115, fou . . . folle . . . fool . . . mad . . . non-sense . . . senselessness: *Mais* fool *ne veut pas dire fou ne veut pas dire* mad *ne veut pas dire fou au sans sens de sans sens.* Cixous executes a highly compressed wordplay here. First, with the French adjective/noun *fou . . . folle*, whose translation into English is usually "mad (madman/madwoman)" or "crazy," could also be "foolish" or "fool," with which it shares a Latin root *follis* (once "a pair of bellows, windbag"). Second, the French locution *veut dire*, usually translated into English as "means," means literally "to want to say," or here, "not to want to say." Finally, *sans sens* means "without sense, without meaning" but could be *heard* as *son sense*, that is, "its sense."

PAGE 116, One male the other female? A fool to say it and a fool to see it? Madman to say it and a madwoman to see it? *L'une male l'autre femelle? Fou de dire et folle de voir?* English has difficulty translating the difference between *fou* ("fool, foolish, mad," in the masculine) and *folle* ("fool, foolish, mad," in the feminine) and the play on words here.

DONNE IS DONE

The French title for this chapter is "Donne donne la Mort."

PAGE 128, Don't forget that I am Jewish *Jewish Jesus*: N'oublie pas que Jésuis juif. The French here and in the following pages plays on the phonic similarity of *je suis* ("I am") and *Jésus*: *Jésuis juif* compacts "I am Jewish" and "Jesus Jewish" into a single enunciation.

PAGE 132. The dungeon: *Le donjon.* In French "gift" is *le don*: the word *donjon* or "dungeon" thus encloses within it the word *don*.

PAGE 1 5 3, locked up: *enfermée*. The word *enfermée* returns in various forms, obsessively, in the following paragraph. It does not, strictly speaking, mean "locked," but "shut" or "closed" up; within itself it encloses the word *enfer* ("hell").

PAGE 1 5 5, kill the silence that is killing me: *tuer le tu qui me tue.* *Le tu* is "the silence" or "the unsaid," but it is also the second person singular (familiar) pronoun "you."

PAGE 1 5 7, my two months': *mes deux moi's)*. The French plays on the homophony of *mes deux moi* ("my two selves") and *mes deux mois* ("my two months").

PAGE 1 6 6, You can tell the genius by *what* he steals. *That* he steals. By his flights of fancy. An idiot thief: he should have flown on his own, robbed himself, had he known: *On reconnait le genie à* ce *qui'il vole. A ce qu'il vole. Un voleur idiot: il aurait dû se voler lui-même. s'il avait su.* Note that *voler* ("to steal") has a homonym, *voler* ("to fly").

PAGE 1 7 1, *Elpenor Queudal* Elpenor Not a Thing: *Elpénor Queudal.* Of obscure origin, *que dal* is a French phrase of negation and refusal, meaning (to understand, see) "nothing . . . not a thing." *Queue* means "tail."

PAGE 1 7 5, Gregor Elpenor Queudal inventor of no-life, says my brother, not bad: *Gregor Elpenor Queudal l'inventeur du pas de vie, dit mon frère, c'est pas mal.* Notice the play, in the French, on the word *pas*, meaning both "nothing . . . not" and "step"; thus *pas mal* means "not bad," but also "bad step."

PAGE 1 8 0, the Fisher King: *le roi Pêcheur.* In French the words *pêcheur* ("fisher") and *pécheur* ("sinner") are almost identical in sound and spelling.

PAGE 182, the imitation squirrel skin slippers: *les pantoufles en imitation vair*. In French, Cinderella's slippers are in *vair*, "squirrel fur." *Verre*, which sounds almost the same, is "glass," a homophony which may explain why Cinderella has a glass slipper in the tale's English version.